CLINT CAIN

The Texan Avenger

Robert Hanlon

FOREWORD
FROM PAUL L. THOMPSON

When it comes to great Western books—and there are a fair few of them out there—it takes a great author to realize the power of action scenes. The action scene is likely one of the most popular parts of the Western, and yet, so many authors fail to deliver on their promises of high-octane powerful action sequences. Robert Hanlon never fails in this regard. When it comes to delivering the best action, Hanlon has the gift.

Not only would I suggest you read this book for the action, I'd suggest you try some of his other books, too. All of them are worthwhile—"Bounty For The Preacher," however, stands as my favorite. I'm sure this new book will become a fast favorite, as well. I'm currently on my second read through and it's already starting to nudge "Bounty For The Preacher" into second place on my personal favorite book chart. Try it—you'll love it, too.

Paul L. Thompson – Bestselling author of the Shorty Thompson, U.S. Marshal series.

CHAPTER ONE

It was a late October afternoon. The sun was waning, and the dinner cooking in the pot on the cook stove was calling them. Clint Cain was happy to be working with his grandpappy, whom he affectionately called Pappy. Pappy had fought in the War Between the States, just as Clint's father had. Pappy raised mules for a living, and Clint enjoyed helping him with them. He also enjoyed learning how to care for and control the mules, and anything else Pappy had a mind to teach him, like how to use a gun.

At sixteen, the blue-eyed, blond-haired Clint was an old hand at wrangling the mules and was planning on taking over the mule business from Pappy in a couple years. It had been Pappy's idea for Clint to take over the mules. Pappy would simply give Clint the farm, and he could provide for Pappy in his old age, in lieu of payment.

It was hard for Clint to think of Pappy as being old. He'd never known him when he was young, but his body seemed to defy his age. At sixty, Pappy was still in prime health. He had a big barrel chest and arms as thick as tree limbs. His hair may have turned gray, but he was just as quick-witted as he had been when he was a youth. Pappy was also a man of few words. He kept to himself, unless he was selling mules or buying supplies.

Clint was out in the corral herding the last of the mules into the barn, when he looked up and saw two men riding hard up the trail that led to Pappy's spread. He didn't like the way they were racing towards them, so he yelled out.

"Pappy, we got strangers coming!"

"How many?" Pappy yelled back.

"Two men on horseback. They're riding hard, too!"

"Come to the barn right now, Clint. Get my shotgun, and be ready. It's hanging on the nail by the second stall," Pappy called out as he grabbed his Winchester that was leaning against the barn wall and cocked it.

From this distance, about a quarter-mile away at the tree line, the men looked almost ghostlike. They rode through the rising heat of the day, their dusters flapping in the wind. As they drew closer, you could see they were road weary. They were dirty, with scraggly beards. Their horses were lathered and panting hard as they entered the barn yard, stopping just short of the barn and Pappy with his Winchester.

"Who are they, Pappy?" Clint asked quietly as the men dismounted and brushed off what trail dirt they could. Pappy didn't answer him. This wasn't the time, nor the place, to explain things.
"Whatever you do, Clint, don't say anything. Let me do all the talking, you hear? And keep that shotgun pointed towards

them, but don't hold it to your shoulder. Hold it at your waist, just like I taught you," Pappy directed. Clint was no stranger to the shotgun, so he did exactly as Pappy instructed.

"Okay, Pappy. I'm ready," Clint said and stood tall next to him.

Clint had never seen men like these two before. They were ragged, tattered, and hollow-eyed. They were both carrying side arms and looked like they knew how to use them. Their eyes were darting about as if they were looking for someone, or something, and trusted no one. They wore trouble like most folks wore hats.

"Howdy, Bear," said the man on the right. He was dressed in a brown slicker with a dark brown hat.

"Cort, been a long time," Pappy replied as he nodded at the other man who was looking around like he was expecting someone else to be there. "Bo, is there something bothering you?" Pappy asked.

"Just some pesky pole cats is all," Bo replied with a slight grin. Bo was a big burly man with a beard as black as molasses.

"What brings you boys by?" Pappy asked.

"Well, we could use some grub and a night's lodging in your barn, if you're obliged," Cort said.

"All right. You boys just passing through?" Pappy asked.

"Good ol' Bear! Direct and to the point!" Bo snarled as he straightened himself in his saddle. Once he was comfortable, he continued, "Yep, just passing through. We'll pull out in the morning."

"That's fine," Pappy answered as if he didn't really have a choice. "Clint, I think it's time for you to head on back to your pa now. It's getting late," Pappy said, trying to get the boy away from the farm.

"But Pappy, I don't have to be back until tomorrow, and I—" Clint started to reply, when Cort interrupted him.

"We'd rather the boy stayed here tonight," Cort said as he stared right at Pappy. "Besides, like he said, he doesn't have to be back 'til tomorrow. Plus, it's safer this way." Pausing for a moment, Cort looked at Clint. "He's a good lookin' kid. Who is he?"

"My grandson, Clint," Pappy proudly stated.

"Is that John's boy?" Cort asked.

"Yep," Pappy answered.

"Well, I'll be. Say, how is John?" Cort continued.

"We'll talk about that later, boys," Pappy curtly replied. He then turned to Clint. "Run to the house and wait for me while I get these men settled in."

"Okay, Pappy," said Clint, and he turned and started walking towards the house. He looked back over his shoulder a half-dozen times as he went, just checking on Pappy.

"Why don't you join us in the barn, Bear? We can catch up on lost time and stay out of view," Bo said as he started walking his horse inside.

As he walked to the house, Clint had lots of questions running through his mind. *Who were these men? How did they know Pa and Pappy? Why were they calling Pappy 'Bear'? Why did Pappy try to get rid of me? Why did he look so worried?* When Clint reached the door, he stopped and turned around to see Pappy and the two men disappear into the barn.

Curiosity got the better of him, and he ran back to the barn. He snuck up to the side of it where he could peek through the boards, and listened in as Pappy and the strangers began talking.

"Sorry the accommodations aren't better, Cort," Pappy said.

"This is just fine. We've slept in worse places," Cort replied. "We appreciate you letting us stay for the night."

"No problem. You know if anyone asks, I haven't seen you," Pappy told them.

"Hell, we know that. That's why we feel safe here," Bo interjected. "Yeah, good ol' Bear. You should've stayed with us after the war. We've had some interesting times, I tell ya."

"Some close calls I hear, too," Pappy countered.

"No closer than the war," Bo said.

"At least in the war, we knew who the enemy was. What you boys face now, you don't know who might pull the trigger, or when, or what corner they might be around," Pappy retorted.

"Sounds like fun, huh, Bear?" Cort said.

"Hell no!" Pappy spat. The two men laughed.

"So, how is John?" Cort asked Pappy.

"We don't speak much. There's some things you don't forgive, I guess." There was a sadness in his voice. "Let's talk about things a little more cheerful," Pappy continued. "Cort, do you still read like you used to?"

"A little. Don't get much time to read a good book these days," Cort replied. "We've been moving around a lot."

Clint was trying to process all he was hearing. He knew that Pa and Pappy were in the war. He knew that Pappy had ridden with Cort James. Heck, the entire county knew that. *Could this be the real Cort James? That would make sense. That's why they're hiding in the barn—it's the outlaw, Cort James, right here at Pappy's farm!*

"So, how's the mule business, Bear?" Cort asked.

"Not bad. Not bad at all, with the sodbusters headed out west. Every one of them needs a good pack mule and a plow mule. Every couple of months, I go to town with a good string and never bring any back," Pappy grinned proudly.

"I guess raising mules beats being shot at," Bo interjected.

"Damn sure does," said Pappy as he rose to his feet. "You boys settle down and relax. I'll go to the house and rustle up some grub and a jug."

Clint jumped up and ran to the house, his heart pounding. He waited in the kitchen for Pappy.

As Pappy approached the house, he thought how much he missed the thrill of the hunt, that walk on the edge. Seeing Cort and Bo, it also reminded him that it was a younger man's game. He'd been the old man of the group even back then, and he hadn't gotten any younger since.

The screen door had barely closed behind him as he entered the house, when Clint, who could hardly contain himself, grabbed him by the arms, looked him in the face, and asked, "Is that Cort James, the outlaw, Pappy?"

"Clint!" Pappy said sternly. "Don't you ever say that name out loud again! Never! And how do you know about him, anyway? Did you sneak back out to the barn? You did, didn't you? I ought to tan your hide. We'll discuss this later, but for right now you've got to stay quiet, you hear? You don't let them know you know who they are, and you don't ever tell anyone they were here. Especially not your pa!" Pappy growled at Clint. "Do you understand, boy?" he asked curtly.

"Not even Pa?" Clint asked for clarity.

"Especially not your pa. There's a lot you don't know, and right now's not the time to discuss it, but we will someday. Someday soon."

"Okay, Pappy, but promise you'll tell me later?"

"I said I would, didn't I? Now you mind me, and stay away from those men unless I'm with you," Pappy ordered.

"Yes, sir, I'll do just that," Clint replied.

The morning sun had barely broken the horizon when Clint's feet hit the floor. He was an early riser and had been his whole life. He liked to get his chores done and then go fishing or hunting the rest of the day, unless he was here, helping Pappy with his mules.

"Rise and shine, Pappy!" he called out cheerfully.

Pappy, startled from his sleep, rolled over and sat up. "Damn, the older I get, the less refreshing sleep is becoming," he groused.

"Are we fixing breakfast this morning?" Clint asked as he looked out the kitchen window towards the barn.

"I'll need to go see if they'll be wanting some before they leave. Get the stove fire burning anyway. At least we'll have breakfast." Pappy pulled on his pants and stumbled out the door to wash his face at the well. When he'd finished, he walked over to the barn, let the mules out into the corral, and walked back to the house.

"Let's rustle up a whole bunch of eggs and bacon. They claim to have been considering eating a mule, just before I got out there," Pappy said, jokingly. After cooking a good solid breakfast of eggs, bacon, and biscuits for their two guests, Pappy and Clint carried two plates out to the barn.

"Good morning," Clint said as he and Pappy entered the barn, trying extra hard to conceal his excitement.

"Morning to you," Cort James said in reply, while Bo just grunted.

While the two men ate, Pappy busied himself feeding the mules. Clint, despite Pappy's orders not to interact with these men, stood there staring at Cort. He was totally starstruck.

"What is it, boy?" Cort asked as he looked up from his plate between mouthfuls of food. "You're eyeballing me awfully hard."

Clint was embarrassed at being caught, but he was also quick-witted. "Excuse me for staring, sir, but I've never seen anyone enjoy Pappy's cooking before," Clint grinned. The two men laughed, and then Cort got serious and gave Clint a hard look.

"How old are you, boy?" Cort asked, his eyes staring at Clint's face.

"Sixteen, sir," Clint answered quietly.

"You're well-mannered, and I like that." Cort continued, "I'm going to tell you something, young man, and I want you to listen. Now, Bear, correct me if I'm wrong..." Cort called out loudly enough for Pappy to hear him. Pappy stopped what he was doing and walked over to Clint.

"Clint, you're almost a man. Hell, I wasn't much older than you when I was whipped like a slave. But you know what? I never cried out. Not once. Don't ever let anyone push you around, young man, and don't cry out and let them think you're weak. You hear me?"

"Yes, sir," Clint replied, suddenly feeling afraid of Cort. He liked the way he had said he was almost a man, but he didn't know why he thought it necessary to talk about being whipped and not crying out.

"The only way to make it in this world is to be tough," Cort said firmly. "Tougher than the other man who's out to get you, to take what's yours. Never give up, and never, ever surrender. Lay low for a spell if you need to rest, but get back up to fight another day. Show no mercy because, boy, they'll show you none… none whatsoever. Keep your friends close and your enemies closer," Cort stated with finality. "Your pappy taught me that at the start of the war. I've never forgotten it, and it's served me well. Now you know it, and it can serve you well, too."

Clint turned and looked at his pappy, then back at the two men who were finishing their meal. Just as he picked up the dishes to take them back to the house, all hell broke loose. Multiple gunshots rang out. What sounded like hundreds of hammers banging on the walls of the barn were bullets exploding through the wooden walls. Splinters rained down on them as the bullets zinged past, sounding like a swarm of angry hornets.

Instantly, Cort and Bo dove to the ground. Pappy shoved Clint down, and then dropped on top of him, covering him with his body, trying to protect him. Then as suddenly as it had started, the shooting stopped. And after a brief moment of silence, a man began talking loudly.

"That was just to get your attention!" the man bellowed from across the barnyard.

"Damn posse!" Cort spat as he and Bo checked their six shooters.

"Now, you boys come on out nice and peaceful like, and no one gets hurt!" the voice continued. Cort looked at Pappy and grinned.

"I hate to eat and run, Bear, but I think management wants us to check out!"

"Where are your horses?" Pappy asked as he looked around for them.

"We put them out back, hidden in a thicket just in case something like this happened," Bo said as he winked at Clint who was still down on the ground. Cort and Bo moved quickly, yet cautiously, to the back of the barn where they had found a small animal door that led to the corral and slipped out.

As they left, Cort looked back and said, "We appreciate the hospitality, Bear. We'll see you again sometime, when we're not so pressed for time. Clint, mind your pappy, and grow up to be a good man, not some low-down criminal like me." With that, he was gone.

"Well, boys! What's it going to be?" the voice demanded.

"Aren't you going to say something, Pappy?" Clint asked.

"In a minute," Pappy answered as he walked slowly towards the big door at the front of the barn. "Bring the dishes with you. Remember, we breakfast out in the barn a lot. That way, we can get a head start on tending the mules. Gives us more time to go fishing in the afternoon," Pappy said. Clint nodded understanding.

"Well, boys, I'm losing patience!" After a brief pause, the man shouted, "Ready, aim…"

"Hold your damn horses, we're coming out! We're unarmed!" Pappy shouted and led the way out of the barn with Clint a step behind him. Pappy had his hands above his head. Immediately a man on horseback, dressed like a dandy in a right nice suit, rode up. He had a six gun, and it was pointed right at Pappy.

"Where are they?" he demanded.

"Where is who?" Pappy replied, stern-faced.

"Search the area, men! They can't have gone far!" the man shouted. Ten men slipped out of the woods and began searching the farm. They went through the house, barn, outbuildings, and even the outhouse, but no one was found, or any trace that anyone but Pappy and Clint had been there.

"You can put that away," Pappy said, pointing to the man's six gun. "We're not armed."

The man ignored Pappy and instead barked at him, "You know damn well who I'm talking about! You used to ride with them," the man said, still aiming his weapon. Then he looked at Clint. "And who the hell are you?"

Pappy interjected before Clint could answer. "My name's William Cain. This here's my grandson, Clint. And you are?" Pappy asked as he stared at the man.

"Mr. Ferguson of the Pinkerton Detective Agency. May I ask you a question, Mr. Cain?"

"You just did," Pappy replied snidely. The look on Mr. Ferguson's face told Clint he was not amused by Pappy's comment. If looks could kill, Pappy was a goner.

"Do you have any idea what those two men have done, Mr. Cain?"

"Can't say I have. Because, after all, I haven't a clue who the hell you're talking about in the first place," Pappy snapped at the man.

"Really?" Mr. Ferguson said. "Aren't you the William 'Bear' Cain who rode with Quantrill's Raiders and personally know Cort James and his cousin, Bo Morgan?"

Pappy began to lose his patience with the man. "If you mean Captain Quantrill—"

"He was captain of what, sir? A bunch of renegades?" Mr. Ferguson barked, interrupting Pappy.

"Now, see here, mister!" Pappy answered back, more than a little perturbed. "You Yankees called us raiders and a lot worse, because you were tired of having your asses kicked by us! And the who hell told you about me? It was long time ago, and the war is over. I gave up riding with Quantrill when the war ended. I was pardoned with the rest of the Confederate Army."

"I'm a Pinkerton detective, and I have ways of finding out lots of things that people would prefer never saw the light of day again. It's my job to know these things. Now, these men whom you don't know and haven't seen, you wouldn't happen to know where they're headed, would you?" Mr. Ferguson asked sarcastically.

"I don't like your tone, sir. If I did know any men you might be after, I'd never tell you a thing," Pappy spat.

"I see. By your answer, it's obvious you're refusing to cooperate. Just a few words of advice. It's not healthy to keep that kind of company around or to lie to the Pinkerton Detective Agency. For your information, I did fight for the Union, and just to remind you, we won. Now, if you'll excuse me I have some outlaws to catch." Mr. Ferguson turned his horse away and started to ride off.

"Not so fast, Mr. Ferguson! You shot several of my mules, and you've got to pay for them!" Pappy shouted after him. Mr. Ferguson pulled up on the reins, turned his horse around, and rode back, stopping just inches from hitting Pappy. Pappy stood his ground, despite the danger of being run down by the Pinkerton man.

"You were harboring fugitives! Whatever happens to you, that's your fault under the law!" the man shouted at Pappy.

"What fugitives? Where are they? Did you see them before you opened fire on my barn, nearly killing me and my grandson? Hell no! I demand you pay for my losses. If you don't, I'll sue Pinkerton's, and I'm sure your bosses won't be too happy to hear how you operate in the field. You'll deny it, of course, but I'll have the evidence! The newspapers won't care and neither will the state's court system. Just the rumor of you being a loose cannon will be bad for business, and you'll be unemployed!" Pappy shouted back.

After a moment, Mr. Ferguson reached inside his coat and pulled out a wallet. He yanked out a handful of money and tossed it at Pappy.

"There! You're compensated! If I hear anything more of it, I'll be back, and I'll have to shoot you for aiding and abetting criminals." The man spat on the ground, then once more turned his horse around and rode off down the trail, with his men following close behind. Pappy and Clint watched the men ride away.

When they were gone, Clint turned to Pappy and asked, "What's a Pinkerton, Pappy?"

"Can't rightly say. Whatever one is, I don't care for 'em," was all Pappy said, then bent down and picked up the money.

"How many mules did they kill?" Clint asked.

"I haven't a clue. I doubt they killed any of them. But they shot the hell out of the barn. We'll be filling holes for weeks just to get it weathertight again."

"How much money did he leave?" Clint asked as Pappy counted it.

"A hundred and twenty dollars, all told."

"Jesus, Pappy! That's twelve mules!" Clint blurted out.

"We'll keep this windfall our little secret, okay, son? I think it's time for you to have your own guns. A Winchester and a Colt Peacemaker... the best there is," Pappy said, smiling at Clint.

"Really, my own guns?" Now it was Clint's turn to smile.

"Let's go get the kitchen squared away. Then we'll skip the chores and go fishing for the day. How's that sound?" Pappy asked, knowing he had just made Clint's day.

"Will you tell me about you and the outlaws, and my father and the war, now?" Clint asked. "After all, don't I deserve to know after I was almost killed for being near them?"

"You deserve to know the truth, but right now we've got this mess to clean up and fish to catch. We'll talk about it while fishing or on the way back home. But never tell your father I told you. He won't be very happy about it. Also, never tell him about what happened here today, or he'll stop you from coming over, and it'll ruin our plans for the future."

"I won't, Pappy," Clint assured him.

"Good man, Clint. Good man."

CHAPTER TWO

Clint's father, John Cain, was a tortured man both physically and mentally. He had nearly lost his leg in the war, and it left him with a severe limp. He was moody, ill, and bad-tempered. He had not always been that way. He had entered the war wanting to be a hero, but all he became was a victim. The war had taken something out of him, and he'd tried to replace it with alcohol ever since. But the more he drank, the meaner he got, and today would be no exception. He made Clint's home life an emotional, mental, and physical epicenter of violence and fear.

Clint arrived home after his afternoon fishing and braced himself for what he knew was coming. He could see it in his father's demeanor. All the way home, he had been hoping that his father would be sober when he arrived, but no such luck. He didn't even say hello as Clint dismounted.

"I've already got the mules hitched up to the plow. You need to get out into the north field," his father told him.

"Yes, sir," said Clint, and he started walking in that direction. He couldn't think of anything worse than staring at a mule's ass all day. He hated farming. For him, farming was like a chicken scratching at the ground for its next meal. He would much rather be at his grandfather's, working with the mules and preparing them for sale. He didn't know what he wanted to do in life, but it sure wasn't going to be a damn farmer. He walked over to where the mules were waiting, took the reins, and began plowing. As he worked the plow, his mind was everywhere but on the work before him. He fantasized about the war and what it must have been like to just travel. He'd never been more than ten miles from home and that had been to sell mules with Pappy when he was twelve. Just the thought of leaving home excited him, but he doubted it would ever happen. He worked the plow until it was too dark to see the rows and then called it a day.

The next morning, Clint was awakened early by his father. His mother had died a few years back of some sort of illness, leaving Clint at the mercy of his father. Luckily, Pappy saw what was happening and took Clint under his wing. He did his best to keep a distance between Clint and his father, Pappy's only son.

"Get up, boy, and go hook up the wagon. We're going to town for supplies," his father said.

As Clint got dressed, yesterday's events swirled in his head, making him dizzy. He wanted so much to share the excitement he had experienced, but he had sworn not to tell. Silence was his only option right now.

"When we get to town, I want you to go over to Mr. Ange's blacksmith shop and get some horseshoe nails," his father instructed him.

"Yes, Pa. How many pounds?" Clint asked.

"What?" his father asked.

"How many pounds of nails should I get?" Clint asked again.

"Don't get smart with me, boy! I'll beat the tar out of you!" his father spat at him.

"I wasn't getting smart with you, Pa. I don't how many nails to get. I was asking you to tell me how many I should buy." Clint did his best to dissuade his father from getting angry and beating him.

"Two pounds," his father replied.

The ride into town was uneventful and silent for the most part. Occasionally, the silence was broken by his father giving Clint directions regarding which road to take and how to drive the wagon, despite Clint having been driving since he was eight or nine years old. The rest of the time, Clint's mind was racing, but he didn't dare ask his father any questions about the war. He was afraid to, and his father had already started drinking. His father was never in a good mood. The only thing Clint remembered from his childhood was the heated discussions among the women and the men too old to fight. They argued about whose side was right or wrong, and they would always drag God into it... as if God picked a side in a war. It made no sense to him. He was young, but he had enough sense to know that God was loving and caring. God would never condone the death of a human at the hands of another. As they entered the little town of Prairie Home, a town only ten years older than Clint, John reminded Clint of his task.

"Run over to the blacksmith shop and get those nails, like I told you."

"Yes, sir," Clint replied as he jumped off the wagon and ran towards Mr. Ange's shop.

"Don't be too long! I'm gonna need you to help me load supplies!" his father hollered.

Clint entered the shop. "Hello, Mr. Ange."

"Well, hello to you too, Clint," Mr. Ange said. "I'll be right with you. I've just got to finish repairing this wheel for these two young men."

Clint waited for his eyes to adjust from the sunshine to the lack of light inside the blacksmith shop. Once they had adjusted, he saw two young men about his age dressed in chaps. They were obviously cowboys.

"Howdy," Clint said to them.

"Howdy," came the reply.

"Are you real cowboys?" Clint asked as though seeing a cowboy in this neck of the woods was an oddity.

"As real as they get," one of the boys replied.

"We don't get too many cowboys in Cooper County," Clint said.

"We can see why. Ain't much here. We can normally handle the repairs on the trail, but this wheel was really damaged and needed a professional. This is the closest blacksmith shop we could find," the same boy told him.

"Where are you headed?" Clint asked.

"Back home to Pike County," one of them answered.

"Where are you coming from?" Clint then asked.

"Sedalia. We just ran a thousand head up there," the same boy answered. Clint's curiosity was piqued. They had been everywhere and more!

"What do you have to do to be a cowboy?" Clint asked. The two young men looked at each other and smiled.

The other boy finally spoke up. "Run away from home."

"Yeah, run away from home. That is, if you've got one to run away from," the first boy interjected. They both chuckled, but there was a haunting sadness in their voices.

Clint turned his attention back to Mr. Ange. "Pa just wants some nails to shoe one of the mules. He said two pounds." Clint was hoping he'd say just go ahead and take them.

"You tell your pa, if he weren't so stingy, I'd come out to the farm and do it right. That way his mules wouldn't keep throwing 'em," Mr. Ange groused at Clint.

"Yes, sir," Clint replied, knowing he'd never say a word to Pa. He didn't have a death wish.

John Cain walked into the Prairie Home General Store to a warm welcome from Linwood, the store's owner. "Howdy, John!"

"Yes, howdy," John mumbled, and got right to the point. "I got a list here. The usual stuff." He handed the list to Linwood.

"Okay, let's see. Yup, got that, got that. I'll fix you right up. Oh boy, that sure was some ruckus over at your pa's place yesterday, yes, sir!" Linwood said, trying to make conversation.

"What ruckus?" John asked, while staring at Linwood.

Linwood looked John straight in the eye and knew that he'd just opened a can of worms he shouldn't have. He busied himself gathering the items that were on the list, but it didn't deter John from wanting the answer.

"What ruckus, Linwood?" John snapped as he grabbed Linwood's arm.

Reluctantly, Linwood explained. "Seems that a posse, headed by some Pinkerton Detective Agency gentleman, flushed out Cort James and Bo Morgan from your pa's barn."

"This was yesterday morning?" John asked, clarifying.

"Yeah, I hear they shot the hell out of the barn. But that's just what I heard. No telling how much of it is true. Probably none of it."

"Who told you the story?" John demanded.

"Now, John, I can see you're getting worked up about this. Obviously, your boy wasn't hurt, and your father wasn't arrested. So how bad could it have been? You know how stories get twisted in the telling. Hell, they probably just stopped by and asked if he'd seen them." Linwood kept trying to downplay it, but John wasn't buying it. He grabbed Linwood by the shirt collar and shoved him against the wall where the canned goods were stored on shelves.

"I'm going to ask one last time. Who did you hear it from?" John demanded.

Linwood gave in. "I went to Lacy's bar last night after closing the store and some men came in. They said they were working for the Pinkerton Detective Agency. They said they followed the trail right into your father's barnyard where they lost the trail. Then they shot up the barn, having seen your father and Clint carry a couple of plates of food out there. Afterwards, they only found your father and Clint in the barn. James and Morgan had given them the slip. They were taking the night off, and they headed out early this morning to try and find their trail again. They were a right talkative bunch, but I guess everyone is after a few drinks." Linwood shared the whole story, leaving nothing out.

The hair on the back of John's neck stood up. He let go of Linwood and started for the door, stopped, turned around, and told Linwood, "Fill my order. I'll be right back." John walked out the door. As soon as he was outside, he bellowed, "Clint!"

Clint came out of the blacksmith shop and headed towards his father. As he walked up the street, he slowed his pace to assess the situation. When he reached his father, the look on his father's face was one of total rage. Clint didn't understand, but that didn't matter. His father grabbed him by the shirt collar, and slapped him across the face so hard, Clint was knocked sideways and fell to the ground, his shirt tearing.

"When were you gonna tell me, boy? When?" John yelled.

"Tell you what, Pa?" Clint asked as he tried to rub the sting out of his face and the blood off his lip and chin.

"Don't play stupid with me, boy! Yesterday, at your grandfather's! James and Morgan, the damned outlaws! Don't play with me, boy! You should have told me! You liar!" John Cain snarled at his son, his rage growing out of control.

"I didn't lie! I just didn't tell you!" Clint yelled in his defense.

John grabbed him by his torn shirt, yanked him off the ground, and slapped him again. This time, Clint staggered backwards. Everything went black for a moment, and he nearly collapsed from the blow.

"Get your damn ass over to the store, and start loading the supplies! I'll deal with you later!" John barked loudly and then turned to the crowd. "What? You got something to say to me? Go to hell! I'll treat my son any way I see fit!" John yelled. The crowd quickly turned and walked away. John didn't care. He didn't socialize with a damn soul in this town, anyway.

"I'll deal with you later," his father said.

Clint knew what that meant. He'd been 'dealt with later' several times before. He'd struggled to walk and breathe for days afterwards. Those were the times his father was just too drunk and blamed Clint for life's troubles. This time, Clint knew, would be worse. His father hated Pappy for whatever happened between them in the war, and the fact that Clint had kept a secret from him was possibly the worse thing Clint could have done.

John Cain had gone to the saloon, had several drinks, and then bought a bottle. The ride home was pure torture for Clint. His father was hitting the bottle harder, not saying a word, but now and then he'd eye Clint and give him a pure evil look. Clint kept his mouth shut out of fear of getting slapped off the wagon. He knew when he got home it would not turn out well. His father was going to beat him with a piece of leather that hung in the barn. He had felt its sting many times before. He remembered what Cort had told him... Be a man. Don't let anyone push you around. Don't show weakness. That made his mind up. Pa had hit him for the last time. This time he would hit back.

As they pulled up to their home, Clint jumped off the wagon.

The horses started at the sudden slack in the reins, and the whole wagon jerked. Clint's father was tossed backwards into the bed of the wagon and he came up, screaming.

"Where do you think you're going, boy? I'm going to find you no matter where you go! You can't escape me!"

"You ain't whooping me!" Clint yelled as he ran into the barn. The only thing Clint could think of was to get away from his father... away from the farm... just away. He was going to get his horse and do just that.

John staggered into the barn as Clint was throwing his saddle on his horse.

"What the hell do you think you're doing, boy? I ain't through with you!" He grabbed for Clint, but Clint ducked and quickly moved away.

The two of them circled each other several times before his father stopped and pushed the horse into Clint, pinning him against the stall wall.

"Got you, you little bastard!" John snarled as he grabbed Clint's left arm and yanked him from behind the horse. He hadn't counted on Clint thinking fast and grabbing the feed shovel off the hook. When Clint cleared the horse, he swung the shovel as hard as he could with one hand. His father didn't react until it was too late to block the blow. The shovel struck him square on the side of the head with a loud thump.

John Cain fell forward and hit the ground. He made no effort to break his fall, and now he just lay there, not moving. Clint stood there, looking down at his father, with the shovel in his hand and fire in his eyes.

His brain was screaming, *"My God, Clint! What have you done?"* He thought his father was dead, but then he heard him groan lightly. For a moment, he considered hitting him again but thought better of it, dropping the shovel.

He quickly went back to securing the saddle on his horse, knowing he had to leave, and quickly. If his father managed to get up before he was gone, he'd get his gun and kill him. He needed his clothes, but there was no time to go to the house. His father groaned a second time, and when Clint looked over he was moving his leg.

I'll go to Pappy's, Clint thought as he climbed into the saddle. Then he had second thoughts. *No, you can't go there. That's the first place he'll look, and you know those two don't get along.* He remembered the young cowboys at the blacksmith's shop. What they had told him had proven to be prophetic… run away from home.

Clint looked back at his father. He wondered if he knew what he was doing. He just knew he couldn't stay here. He turned his horse around and headed away from his father's farm, never looking back. He had one stop to make. His pappy had promised him something, and it was now time to make good on that promise.

Robert Hanlon

CHAPTER THREE

Just as Pappy was stepping out of the house, he saw Clint riding up. He stopped and stared at the boy. Right away, he knew something was wrong. Clint wasn't supposed to come back for three days.

"What happened to you?" Pappy asked as he spied his torn shirt. "I heard in town what happened. I'm sorry, Clint. I should never have told you not to tell your father," Pappy apologized.

"That's okay, Pappy. He would have hit me anyway when he found out. You know how he is," Clint replied. Clint got quiet for a moment.

"What is it, boy?" Pappy asked.

Clint looked away and then back, his eyes not quite meeting Pappy's. "I almost killed Pa," he said, his voice cracking slightly as he said it.

"You almost did what?" Pappy asked.

"I hit him with a shovel. He was going to beat me. I couldn't let him do that! I didn't kill him, but I thought I had."

Pappy rubbed his face with his hand, while he gave the situation some thought. "You can move in here. We'd always planned on that in a couple of years, anyway. We'll just make the move a little sooner," Pappy told him. "We'll deal with your father when we have to."

"No, Pappy. I won't be his excuse to shoot you. He hates you enough already. If I stay here, he'll kill you," Clint told him.

"Then what do you intend to do?" Pappy asked. "Where are you going to go?"

"I've decided to go to Sedalia," Clint replied.

"Sedalia? What the hell for, boy?"

"I'm going to be a cowboy," Clint declared.

"A cowboy? What in tarnation do you know about being a cowboy?" Pappy shot back.

"About as much as I know about anything else except mule training… nothing. But I'm a quick learner," Clint offered.

"Yeah, right you are. Besides, you've always been a wanderer. I can remember your ma tying you up to the water pump to keep you from disappearing on her," Pappy said, sharing a happy memory, something he rarely did.

"Pappy, please tell me about you and Pa, the war, what happened and all. You promised you'd tell me. I've got to know before I leave." Clint suddenly put Pappy on the spot.

Pappy got a faraway look in his eyes, sighed, and sat down on the steps of the porch.

"Come over here, and sit down, boy," Pappy beckoned. Clint quickly hopped off his horse, trotted over to the porch, and sat down next to his grandfather.

Pappy began, "I rode with a bunch of fellas in the war who didn't exactly follow the rules of civilized combat. We conducted what they called guerilla warfare and fought using Indian tactics. We attacked and killed the enemy anywhere we found them and every chance we got—"

Clint quickly interrupted him. "You, and those men that stopped by here yesterday?"

"Yeah, and a bunch more like them. Now be quiet, and let me tell the story."

"Sorry," Clint mumbled, and sat back to listen.

"One day, we had us a little tussle with some Yankees who had gotten separated from their unit. Licked 'em pretty good. We were scouring the battle scene and searching the bodies, looking for anything we could use. You know… food, weapons, ammunition, whatever we could find. We didn't get our supplies from the regular army. Hell, we weren't even recognized by the regular army! Anyway, we came across this one soldier who was hurt pretty badly. His leg was damn near blown off. Cort drew his gun to kill him."

"Why was he going to kill him? He was already hurt," Clint asked, unable to help himself.

"Dead men are easier to steal from," Pappy explained coldly.

"Oh," Clint said, not sure he liked that side of his pappy.

"Anyway, I placed my hand on Cort's weapon and made him lower it. Cort looked at me and asked what the problem was. I told him... " Pappy hesitated a moment, then continued, "I told him that was my son."

"Pa? Pa was a Yankee, and Cort was going to kill him?" Clint blurted out.

"Yes. Your pa was a Yankee. The war had divided us from the beginning. Anyway, I got down off my horse and tried to do what I could for him, but he didn't want any part of it. We heard Union soldiers approaching, so I had to leave him there. If I stayed, I would have been captured, and I knew too much. Besides, Captain Quantrill would never have let that happen. He would have killed both of us first. I'll never forget the way your father looked at me as I rode away." Clint could hear the sadness in his pappy's voice.

"Now you know. Now you know why your father hates me. Rightfully so, I guess. We all lost something in that war. Your father lost the use of his leg, and I lost my son." Pappy stopped talking, and he and Clint sat there in an eerie silence for several minutes, until finally, Pappy spoke up.

"I saw how you looked at Cort and Bo. Don't you think for one minute they're heroes, Clint. A lot of men did what they did during the war. That doesn't make them heroes. War is where losers die, and there are no winners. What they do now is for a completely different reason, and that reason ain't a good one. Do you understand?" Pappy asked.

"Yes, Pappy, I think so," Clint assured him. When Clint looked up, he saw tears in his pappy's eyes, and his face was a mask of profound sadness. Pappy realized that Clint was looking and quickly wiped his tears away.

"Before you go," Pappy said, "I have something to give you." He gathered himself as he stood up. Clint watched him disappear into the house. A moment later, he stepped back out onto the porch. He was a carrying a gun belt with two Colt pistols in it and a box of ammo. "I wore these in the war," he said as he handed them to Clint.

"Why did you carry two guns, Pappy?"

"Because they kept me balanced. I haven't worn them since the war. You might need 'em. Whatever you do, don't make me regret giving 'em to you. In other words, I don't want to have to bury you because I gave them to you. You understand?" Pappy asked sternly.

"I understand, Pappy. You don't have to worry. I won't kill anyone, and I won't let anyone kill me," Clint replied, strapping them on.

"Good boy. Oh, here's some money, too. You can't get too far without money. I wish it was more," he said as Clint looked at the money. It was a hundred dollars.

"But Pappy, this is the money from the Pinkerton man," Clint pointed out.

"Yep. I don't need it. All the mules are fine," Pappy replied. Clint just stood there looking at him. Now the tears were welling up in his eyes, too.

"You'd best go before your pa shows up, or I talk you out of going," Pappy told him through a clenched jaw as a tear leaked down his cheek. "Don't you forget your old pappy now, you hear. Stop by when you can. Now get!" Pappy tried to sound tough, but failed and stood there crying.

"I won't ever forget you, Pappy. I love you," Clint said with a trembling voice as he hopped on his horse. He took one last look back, kicked his horse, and galloped away.

CHAPTER FOUR

Clint rode all that evening, watching the sky change colors. Pink fingers of orange, red, and yellow streaked across the sky as the sun said goodbye to another day. He rode on into the darkness, and he couldn't have picked a better night to ride. The fall air was cool, the moon was full, and there wasn't a cloud to be seen. The stars shone through the black velvet sky as if God had used a pin to prick holes through the purple blanket, letting his light shine through to guide Clint on his way. Clint had no idea what his future held. He just knew he had to move forward. There was no going back.

After riding for several days, eating only what he hunted, Clint spotted a large dust cloud in the distance.
He quickened his pace and soon saw what was raising such a dust cloud. It was a herd of cattle being driven across a dry valley. Along the outside edges were several riders… cowboys. Near the front were three cowboys in a cluster, looking his way. One broke rank and started towards Clint. He was trotting along at a leisurely pace, and Clint rode over to meet him. The cowboy stopped about a dozen yards shy of Clint, resting his hand on his pistol. Seeing that, Clint stopped and raised his hands. "Howdy, I'm Clint Cain."

This cowboy was nothing like the two young men Clint had met at the blacksmith shop. He was older, much older, and rugged looking. He was the kind of man you automatically knew not to mess with.

"Why are you following us?" he asked curtly. Clint was stunned. He didn't know what to say. "Well, boy? Cat got your tongue?"

"I was just... I..." Clint stammered.

"Well, spit it out, boy! I ain't got all day!" the man snarled at Clint.

"I want to be a cowboy!" Clint finally blurted out and sat, looking hopeful.

The man seemed to be amused by Clint's comment. "Son, you ain't even big enough to be a man, much less a cowboy! Best you go on back where you came from. This land has a way of swallowing up people like you, never to be heard from again. Do you want your mother waiting for a letter that will never come? Want to be buried in some unmarked grave? I suggest you stop following us. Now get!" the man barked. He turned his horse around and rode away.

Clint sat there, not knowing what to do. He couldn't go home. Pa would certainly kill him now, if he did. Not only would he be a failure, he'd be a dead failure. He kept his distance but continued to follow the cattle drive the rest of the day. That night, he watched their campfire from a distance. He was cold, alone, tired, and discouraged. He cried himself to sleep.

The next morning, Clint decided the only choice he had was to keep following the drive from a good distance. If nothing else, they would lead him into Sedalia. Towards the end of the day, through the twilight, he could see the town. As he rode in, he noticed the number of buildings, the water troughs, and the boardwalks. He had never seen a town this big before. He was looking for a livery stable and didn't have to go far. Just ahead of him was the orneriest looking man he had ever laid eyes on, standing under a sign that said: 'The Green Livery Stable.' The man looked at Clint with eyes that bore right through him.

"Well, what the hell do you want?" the man cussed.

"I need to bed down my horse for the night," Clint replied, trying not show how scared he was.

"That will be two bits... three, if you want him hayed," the man stated curtly.

"Sir?" Clint asked.

"What?" the man asked in reply, running out of patience.

"I don't have a lot of money," Clint said as he dismounted.

"Well, ain't nothing here for free. Not even the clap." The man spit a cob of chewing tobacco on the ground. Clint wasn't sure what the man meant, so he ignored the comment and said, "Well, sir, I was thinking—"

"Thinking what?" the man interrupted, staring at Clint with a snarl on his face.

"I was thinking, if you let me stay in the stable, too... I mean, for the three bits, I could clean the stalls and all, to pay my way," Clint quickly stammered to be sure he said it all before the man interrupted him again.

"Let me guess," the man said, scratching his head. "You're a milk fed sodbuster from Oklahoma whose father beat you. Your mother was a whore, and you've decided to run away from home to become a cowboy. Is that about right?"

"Well, not exactly, sir. I'm from Missouri, and my mother was a lady before she passed away."

"Not exactly?" he said, sounding sarcastic. "Hell, all right. But let me tell you one thing. Those stalls better be so clean in the morning I could eat off them, you got me?"

"Yes, sir," Clint replied, smiling.

"Well, go on. Put up your mount. You can sleep in the loft of the barn," the man said.

"Thank you, sir," replied Clint as he started for the barn, pulling his horse along by the reins.

"Pay me first, and then you can thank me," the man said, stopping Clint in mid-stride. Clint turned away slightly from the man, not wanting him to see just how much money he had, and pulled the three bits out of his pocket. He gave the man his money, walked his horse into the stable, and looked around. He clearly had his work cut out for him. He reached into his saddlebag, took out his last two biscuits and his canteen of water, and ate his meager meal before setting to work on cleaning the stalls.

In the morning, the man opened the barn door and stepped inside, where he exclaimed, "What the hell?"

Clint raised his head from the loft to look down on the stable owner standing in the middle of the barn, hands on his hips, looking around in amazement. Every tool was in its place. Every piece of tack was cleaned and put away. The hay was perfectly stacked. The stalls were immaculate.

"Boy, get down here!" the man bellowed. Clint rubbed the sleep from his eyes and climbed down the ladder. "What's your name, son?"

"Clint, sir. Clint Cain."

"Well, Clint Cain, it takes a lot to impress me, but I am truly impressed. Oh, by the way, my name is Mr. Green. Lewis Green." The man was considerably nicer this morning than last night. Clint's hard work had completely disarmed the man of his ill temper. He stuck out his hand, and Clint shook it vigorously.

"Good to meet you, Mr. Green."

It's a pleasure to meet you, Clint. You know, I really didn't expect to find you here this morning. No, sir, sure didn't," Mr. Green said.

"Well, sir, my pappy told me you could tell the character of a man by the way he keeps his barn, and the way he keeps his word. Not saying that there was anything wrong with your barn to begin with, mind you."

"Your pappy sounds like a wise man, Clint."

"He is, Mr. Green, he is."

"Say, how would you like to join me and the missus for breakfast?"

Clint wasn't a big fan of breakfast, but after three days of dry biscuits and squirrel, a hot meal sounded really good. "Yes, sir! Thank you, sir!"

They all sat at the breakfast table with Mrs. Green giving the blessing. Mrs. Green reminded Clint of his mother, but older. They enjoyed the normal chit chat but eventually the conversation got around to Clint. He didn't go into any detail, just telling them that he was restless, wanted to see the world, and that he really wanted to be a cowboy.

"I might be able to help you out there, Clint," Mr. Green said. "There's a ranch owner that just happens to be in town selling a herd of cattle right now. He usually sells me some of his riding stock before he leaves to go back to Texas. Would you like to meet him?"

"Sure would!" Clint replied, smiling.

"Okay. After I straighten up the stable... Oh, wait a minute, that's already done. What do you say we head on over there right now?"

"I'm game. Thank you for breakfast, Mrs. Green," Clint said, following his mother's training and being polite.

"You're more than welcome, Clint. Good luck, and may God bless you," Mrs. Green told him as he and Mr. Green walked out the door.

"Thank you again," Clint said as the door closed.

CHAPTER FIVE

The telegram from Chicago read as follows:

Colonel Billups. Stop. Do not ship cattle until further notice. Stop. Chicago on fire. Stop. No trains in or out. Stop. Will contact later. Stop.

"Now what the hell am I supposed to do?" Colonel Roman Billups growled as he stood in the railway messenger's office after reading the telegram.

"I've got fifteen hundred head of prime beef out there in pens I can't send to Chicago, and I'm supposed to just sit here? How in the hell is an entire city on fire? I can't afford to feed them while we wait for it to stop burning! They'll drop weight fast if I don't feed them, and that's not good, either," the colonel lamented out loud as he paced the floor.

Colonel Billups was an ex-Union army officer, a man of action with a fighting spirit. Although he was middle-aged, he bore an aura of physical power. He was strongly built, above average height, fit and trim.

"Well, Colonel, I did hear there's a purchasing agent representing a gentleman by the name of Jake Hill who's buying beef to feed the Indians and soldiers out west. But that would mean moving them to Fort McPherson, Nebraska, another three hundred and fifty miles and another three weeks on the trail. That is, if the weather holds up," Mr. Pratt informed his boss.

Mr. Pratt was the first sergeant for Colonel Billups during the war. His face had a hundred trails etched in it. He was a no-nonsense man with discipline ingrained in him. He was resilient, steadfast, loyal, and always had the colonel's best interests in mind. They were like brothers and even argued like brothers at times.

Just at that moment, Mr. Green walked in with Clint in tow.

"Hello, Colonel! Mr. Pratt! They told me at the hotel I'd find you here at the telegraph office," Mr. Green greeted.

"Yeah, I'm here, all right. Wish I was on my way back to Texas with a wad of money in my pocket. I won't be having any horses for you this time, Lewis. Looks like I'm going to be needing them," the colonel said.

"Sorry to hear that. What's wrong?" Mr. Green asked.

"Seems something's trying to keep me here. What can I do for you?" the colonel asked.

"Will you be needing cowboys? Or do you have enough men?" inquired Mr. Green.

"Maybe, if I can't find all of them that I came here with. I was foolish enough to loan a few of them some money. They're probably drunk or shacked up with a painted lady right now, or both. Why do you ask?"

"Well, this young man is looking for a job," Mr. Green said as he presented Clint. "Now, you know me. I wouldn't recommend him if I didn't know he's a hard worker. His name is, well, go ahead, tell them your name, son."

Clint took a step forward and introduced himself. "Hello, sir, my name is Clint Cain."

"You're mighty young, son. How old are you?" the colonel asked.

"Sixteen, sir," Clint stated boldly.

"Hey, you're that kid that was following us on the way in, aren't you?" Mr. Pratt said, eyeing Clint.

"Yes, sir," Clint said, recognizing the man as the one who told him to go home. Clint swallowed hard.

"You ever cowboyed before, young man?" the colonel asked.

"No, sir. But I've worked with, corralled, and broken in mules," Clint stated proudly.

"I don't know…" the colonel hesitated. "We just might have a long way to go and a short time to get there. I'm going to need experienced men," he said, dismissing Clint. But Mr. Pratt was studying Clint. He saw something in him he liked.

"You know, Colonel, we could use a new wrangler." The colonel looked at Mr. Pratt and, knowing him, got the hint.

"I'll tell you what. I wouldn't normally hire a greenhorn, but if Mr. Green here is as good a judge of character as he is horseflesh, I guess you've got a job. But, if you think for one moment that going on the trail is fun and safe, you might as well stay here," the colonel informed Clint.

"Thank you, sir!" Clint exclaimed excitedly, a huge grin on his face.

"Don't thank me yet, son. You might be cussing me out before all of this is over," replied he colonel. "Now, where is this purchasing agent, Mr. Pratt?"

"He's in Abilene. I've already wired him and told him of our predicament. He said he'd meet the Chicago price. Wants to know how soon we can leave. I just need the okay from you," Mr. Pratt replied.

"You think you're always one step ahead of me, don't you?" The colonel eyed his trail boss, foreman, and best friend.

"Not always. Besides, I'm just doing my job," Mr. Pratt replied, with just a bit of sarcasm.

"Then go ahead. Wire him, and let him know we'll be pulling out tomorrow," the colonel said. Mr. Pratt wrote the message and handed it to the telegraph operator.

"Come on, kid. Follow us," the colonel said, looking at Clint.

"Yes, sir!" Clint then turned to Mr. Green. "Thank you so much for your help."

"Don't make me look bad. Do a good job," Mr. Green said and shook Clint's hand. Clint turned and walked away with the colonel and Mr. Pratt.

"Son, there's no need to call me sir. We're not in the military, and I'm not your father," the colonel said.

"Yes, sir! I mean, yes, Colonel!" Clint stumbled over the words. He wasn't used to addressing his elders in such a familiar way. "Thank you so much! I won't let you down." Clint could hardly contain himself.

"You can stop thanking me. Just do a good job. That'll be all the thanks I need," the colonel told him.

"I will, sir. I will," Clint promised.

CHAPTER SIX

It wasn't the nicest hotel. The lobby was sparsely
accommodated, the carpet stained, and
the place had a musty smell to it. It was also the first hotel
Clint had ever been in. He was mesmerized
as he and the colonel walked through the door.

"Where are you staying, Clint?" the colonel asked.

"I spent last night in the stables," Clint said absently, looking
around in awe.

"The stables? No wonder you stink like a pole cat! You go
over there to the front desk, and tell them that you're staying
as my guest. They'll fix you up with a room," the colonel told
him.

"I don't have any money, Colonel," Clint said, despite having
a hundred dollars in his boot.

"Didn't I say to tell them you're my guest?" the colonel
repeated. "We'll settle up at the end of the drive, provided you
make it to the end. So, get yourself a room and a bath and
plenty of rest tonight. We'll be starting early in the morning."
The colonel then turned to Mr. Pratt. "Go up and tell the men,
the ones you can find anyway, that there's been a change of
plans. Then have them meet us in the saloon in an hour."

"Yes, Colonel," Mr. Pratt said as he headed upstairs.

"Where's your gear? Do you have a change of clothes?" the colonel asked Clint.

"Yes, sir. My belongings are at the stables," Clint replied, then backtracked and said, "Sorry, Colonel."
He stood there, waiting for his next instruction.

"Well, go on. Just don't stand there. Get your stuff," the colonel said, motioning towards the door with his hand. Clint headed out the front door and ran towards the stables as fast as he could. He returned to the hotel a few minutes later carrying his gear and approached the front desk.

"May I help you, young man?" the middle-aged clerk asked.

"Yes, sir. The colonel said to tell you that I'm here as one of his guests," Clint informed him.

"I see," the clerk said as he opened the ledger and ran his finger down the page. "Let's put you in room 203, with a Mr. Cole." He handed Clint a key.

"Don't you want my name?" Clint asked.

"It doesn't matter, son. Hardly anyone here uses their real name anyway," the clerk explained.

Clint climbed the stairs and found the room without any
trouble. He inserted the key and opened it. Immediately,
someone inside the room bellowed, "Who the hell are you,
and what are you doing in my room?" On the bed was a
young man, aiming a pistol at Clint.

"I'm Clint. Clint Cain. The colonel sent me. He... he hired me
as the new wrangler, and the desk clerk sent me up here."
Clint spoke quickly, not wanting to get shot.

"No shit!" the guy on the bed said as he stood up and walked
over to Clint. "Well, my name is Cole. I'm the colonel's
broncobuster and probably the best cowboy he has. Glad to
meet you," he said as he tucked the gun in his holster and
then stuck out his hand.

Clint cautiously shook hands. "Glad to meet you," Clint
responded. He stood in the doorway, unsure what he should
do next.

"Hey, stow your gear over by the window, and take the bunk
on the left," Cole directed.

Clint would come to know Cole well. He was twenty-one, and
wise for his age. He had blond hair, blue eyes, and was of
average build. He was full of himself, crude, and drank too
much. Overall, Cole wasn't too smart. He never knew his
father, and his mother was a barroom whore.

"So, you're the new wrangler. Have you ever worked horses before?" Cole asked.

"No, just mules," Clint offered.

"Mules? Damn, ain't they part jackass?" Cole said, laughing. "Hey, wanna go have some fun later? After our meeting with the colonel."

"What kind of fun?"

"Well, considering your state of appearance and all, I figured you'd get a bath, and we'd go downstairs and have a couple of drinks. It can get pretty lively in here at times."

"I don't know. The colonel told me to get a good night's sleep 'cause we're leaving really early." Clint had never had a drink in his life, although he had seen firsthand what it had done to his father. He gave a halfhearted smile.

"Yeah, I heard. Three more weeks on the trail. Another reason to drink. Now go. Get cleaned up!" said Cole.

"I don't have any money to drink," Clint said, desperately trying to get out of it.

"That's okay, I've got you covered," Cole told him.

"Kind of early to start drinking, ain't it?" said Clint. He really didn't want to go drinking.

"When you drink as much as I do, Clint, you gotta start early." Cole grinned.

CHAPTER SEVEN

The rest of the day was a blur for Clint. He had a quick bath, met with the colonel, had his first drink and several more… Well, he thought there had been several more, but it might have been a dozen or so. The next morning, there was a loud knock on their door. Hell, it was more akin to a mule kicking out the side of a barn.

"We're awake!" Cole yelled and promptly rolled over, pulling the blanket over his head.

Clint opened his eyes and tried to focus, but no such luck. It was all a blur. At the same time, he tried to shake the cobwebs out of his brain, which only made the room spin.

Cole tossed off the covers, looked over at Clint, and started to chuckle.

"What's so funny?" Clint asked. The sound of his own voice hurt his ears.

"Damn, Clint! You look like something that fell out of the ass end of a cow!" Cole tried to stifle his laughter.

Clint was not amused. His head hurt, he felt sick, and he wasn't sure where he was or who the laughing asshole across the room was. Then he remembered he had to start work today and thought this wasn't going to be good.

"Come on, cowboy. The rodeo is about to begin," Cole told him as he jumped out of bed and started to get dressed.

Clint rolled out of bed just as his memory started coming back. Last night. *Oh, my God! Last night.* He could vaguely remember Cole helping him up the stairs. And some woman grabbing at his crotch, her breast nearly hanging out of her dress. *Oh, my God! What had I done?*

"Clint, stop lollygagging. Get dressed. The colonel doesn't like us to be late," Cole said. It sounded as if Cole was yelling at the top of his lungs. It took Clint another five minutes to pull on his clothes, discreetly making sure his money was still in his boot, and not throwing up. Then he and Cole met up with Mr. Pratt down at the holding pens, ready for work.

"Clint, you look a little green this morning. You okay?" Mr. Pratt asked, holding back a smirk.

"I'm all right... I think," Clint mumbled.

"Look, not that I doubt your ability to handle the remuda, but I want you to saddle up and show me that you can," Mr. Pratt told him.

"Sure thing, Mr. Pratt. Ahh... what's a remuda?" Clint asked, sheepishly.

Cole laughed out loud, which drew a stern look from Mr. Pratt. Cole quickly choked the laugh off.

"That's the horses we'll be using on the drive, son," Mr. Pratt told him.

"Oh," Clint said and turned towards the pen with the horses in it. There was a saddle on the fence rail by the gate, and he grabbed it as he walked by. He saddled his horse and was mounted and back at the gate in short order.

"Here's what I want you to do," Mr. Pratt began. "Take these horses from this corral and move them over to that one without getting off your mount."

"Will do," Clint replied and went to work.

Clint moved the herd with ease. He had done the same thing with his grandfather's mules so many times, there was nothing to it. Mr. Pratt was impressed.

"Good job, Clint. You are now the official wrangler for this drive. Here, you're going to need this," he said, handing Clint a rag of some sort.

"What's this?" Clint asked as he stared at it.

"A bandana. You can't be a cowboy without one," Mr. Pratt told him.

"Why do I need a bandana? What do I do with it?" Clint asked.

"It's the official flag of a cowboy! It keeps the sun off your neck and the dust out of your face. It can be used as a wash cloth or a bandage. You can strain sand from your food, form a noose for hanging rustlers, or wear it as a blindfold. Plus, if you happen to die out there, we'll cover your face with it." Clint took it, tied it around his neck, and imagined it over his face. It wasn't a pleasant thought.

Clint had never seen anything like the drive. Fifteen hundred head of cattle was an awesome, and yet terrifying, sight. Even at this slow, meandering pace, if it weren't for the skill of the cowboys wrangling the herd, it would have been total chaos as the cattle were herded out of town. The ground shook beneath him. As they pulled out onto the range, the herd looked like a headless snake with its tail disappearing into a cloud of dust a half-mile behind them.

They drove the herd northwest, crossing through vast seas of grass so tall it polished their boots. After several hours, Clint began to realize that there was no contentment on the trail and very little fulfillment. He had envisioned a glamourous life as a cowboy, but that thought dissipated with every mile that passed. There was nothing romantic about eating dust all day. But, no matter how hard it got, the feeling of freedom it gave him was well worth it. There was something about sitting on a horse and looking down on the world that made him feel alive.

By early evening, the herd had caught up to the chuck wagon that had gone ahead to prepare supper for the day. The men, tired from a long day in the saddle, 'punching cows,' as they say, dismounted and staggered over to the chow line. Clint watched them and realized they all had the same pathetic walk. Stiff and sore from sixteen hours in a saddle, they walked bowlegged. They were dusty, dirty, hungry and thirsty. They worked furiously to set up camp. Tents went up and campfires were built. After everything was done, some of the cowboys walked and stretched their legs. Others stooped by the fires while some worked on their gear. Others just rested. The horses and cattle waited for the cool of the night.

"Clint! Cole! Front and center!" Mr. Pratt called out.

"Yes, sir?" Clint and Cole walked up and answered at the same time.

"Cole, I want you to show Clint how to make a temporary corral before chow," Mr. Pratt said.

"Will do. Come on, greenhorn," Cole said. "Grab a couple coils of that rope off the supply wagon," he directed Clint as he walked off towards an area with a few scrub bushes.

"Take and tie one end of the rope to one of the bushes," Cole instructed, and the rest was easy. They stretched out the rope, tying it off to several of the bushes, making a somewhat circular corral in no time.

When they had finished, Clint began asking Cole some questions.

"How long have you been a cowboy?" Clint asked.

"A few years."

"How'd you get started?"

"Now, that's an interesting story," Cole began. "I was about fourteen and living in a saloon."

"In a saloon?" Clint questioned.

"Yeah. You see, my ma had been a saloon girl, and my pa was a gambler. Pa was killed during a card game. After he died, my ma gave me his guns. See here, my pa's name is engraved on the barrel." Cole pulled out one of his pistols and showed it to Clint.

"Is your ma still alive?" Clint asked.

"No, she died a few months after my pa. Doctor said she had some kind of disease called consumption. I stayed at the saloon and was taken care of by the other women who worked there. I would wander around in the saloon and occasionally pick up a dollar here and there. Drunk people are easy to steal from. One night, the colonel was in the saloon, and he caught me trying to take some money off his table. He gave me the choice of being turned into the sheriff or going to work for him. I wasn't about to go to jail, so here I am. I'm glad I did it. It sure beats stealing. He tried me on that book learning stuff, but I ain't interested in that sort of thing. I just like being a cowboy. So, that's the story. Now, let's go eat."

"Line up, boys!" Dusty, the cook, bellowed as he beat a metal rod on the triangle.

Clint and Cole walked over and joined the grub line. Dusty was a permanent employee of the colonel, much like Mr. Pratt was. He was a veteran cowboy who had gotten too old to work the herd, but he loved the trail. He also acted as the drives' barber, doctor, dentist, and blacksmith. He was a big man, round and jovial, with a mischievous grin, and a demeanor to match. He was also crazy as hell.

When Clint reached the front of the line, Dusty looked up. "Hey!" he said, looking at Clint, "you're the young greenhorn the colonel was telling me about."

"Yes, sir, I guess so," Clint replied.

"Well, I'm Dusty. Pleasure to meet you, young man."

"A pleasure to meet you too, sir."

"Sir? Who are you calling sir? I ain't no rich man. Don't be so polite. I'll give you a couple of days and you'll be cussing and ornery as hell, just like the rest of us! Yep. After two or three days of dirt, dust, and cattle farts, you'll be one of us!"

Clint smiled at him.

"Hold on, young man. You're going to need plenty of strength, so I'm going to make sure you get plenty to eat. We'll fill out that scrawny bag of bones of yours and make a real man and a cowboy out of you," Dusty commented as he heaped a double helping of chow onto his plate. "Now you eat all of that," he ordered as Clint walked away.

Clint sat down by the fire with the rest of the crew and looked at the concoction on his plate. He couldn't tell exactly what he was about to eat. He took a sip of coffee and was surprised at how strong it was.

"Dusty," Clint called out as he went back to staring at the grub on his plate, "my pappy said it's not so important to know what you're eating, but it is important to know what it was before it died. What's in this?"

"Why, I call that my 'son of a bitch' stew," Dusty said. "It's got every part of the steer in it except the hooves and the hide. Hell, you stir it around enough, and you might find an asshole!" Clint looked at Dusty, who was grinning widely.

"I'm just kidding, son. I save the asshole to put on the biscuits in the morning," Dusty teased, and a loud chuckle arose from the other men around the fire. Just then, the colonel approached and walked up to Clint.

"So, how was your first day on the trail?" he asked.

"Well, I thought it might break me, but I'm not broke yet," Clint answered with a grin.

"Good. Did you have any problems handling the horses?"

"No, sir, Colonel. They're a lot easier than mules once you get them pointed in the right direction," Clint shared.

The colonel paused a moment, then fixed his eyes on Clint, making him a bit uncomfortable. "I understand you didn't feel well this morning," the colonel said.

"No, sir, I didn't. I found out that whiskey, early mornings, the smell of cattle, and the hot sun don't mix well," Clint admitted.

The colonel chuckled. "First time drinking?"

"Yes, sir. And it will be a long while before it happens again, if at all."

"That would be a good move. May I give you some advice, Clint?"

"Sure thing, Colonel."

"I know you'll only be on the trail for several weeks, but when you're on it, you've got to buddy up with someone. Someone who will keep your spirits up and keep you going when things get tough."

"Okay. You mean like Cole?" Clint asked.

"Well, Cole's a good cowboy. One of the best. Good to have as a friend on the trail. But off the trail? He's as useless as a bent horseshoe and trickier than a redheaded woman. He can get you into all kinds of trouble. I don't want that for you. Do you?" the colonel asked.

"No, sir."

"Clint, since we're talking and all… I know it's none of my business, and I don't normally ask my employees about their personal lives but… may I ask you a question?"

"Sure, Colonel."

"How is it that a young, good-looking man like yourself ended up out here? I mean, riding on a cattle drive? You look suited for more important work like accounting or such." No one had inquired about Clint's life before, especially anyone like the colonel. Strangely, even though he'd just met the man, he felt he could trust him, so he told him the entire story about his childhood—his mother passing, his father and his drinking, the feud with Pappy, everything. Colonel Billups's heart went out to Clint. Here was a young man who had been emotionally and physically abused by his own father and, out of fear of him, was forced to leave his home. Yet he was still full of hope. When he had finished, Clint had questions of his own.

"May I ask you a question, Colonel?"

"I guess that's only fair. Go ahead."

"Were you a real colonel? What I mean is, did you fight in the war?"

"Yes, I was a colonel in the Union army. But no, I didn't fight in the war. I'm originally from Virginia. I retired about a year before the fighting started. I saw it coming, and I also knew the south would lose the war."

"The north had better soldiers?" Clint asked.

"Oh, no, the north didn't have better soldiers. You see, the north had the factories and the industry. While the south was producing cotton, the north was making munitions like guns and
cannons. I was also personally divided, much like my state. I couldn't choose between two causes so dear to me, one being the army, the other my home. When you do that, you're going to betray one of them. So I sold my property, freed my slaves, and moved to Texas. I got called all kinds of names, but it didn't bother me. Time proved I was right. I later found out

that the Union army burned my old home and scorched the crops. My own army did that." Clint saw that same faraway look in the colonel's eyes that pappy had.

Just at that moment, Mr. Pratt walked up. "I've got the boys all lined up for the watch tonight, Colonel. Clint, you've got the midnight to three shift, so you'd better bed down early."

"Okay, Mr. Pratt. What will I do on the watch?"

"Same thing you do during the day. You'll guard the horses and cattle and keep them calm."

"I can do that," Clint replied and got up to wash his plate and utensils.

"What was that conversation all about, Colonel?" Mr. Pratt asked.

"Oh, just getting to know the boy."

Mr. Pratt had seen that look on the colonel's face before and had heard that tone of voice.

"Colonel, you aren't thinking what I think you're thinking, are you? You know how well that went last time," Mr. Pratt reminded him.

"Cole was a lack of good judgment on my part, Mr. Pratt. Clint is different. He has a heart and is naturally inquisitive.

He questions everything, and if he doesn't like the answer, he questions it again. I like that about him," the colonel replied.

"Oh, Lord, here we go again," quipped Mr. Pratt.

"Keep an eye out for him, will you, Pratt?"

"Sure. Anything you say, boss," Mr. Pratt replied as he walked away to continue his evening checklist. As he walked, he muttered to himself, "I started the day as the trail boss, now I'm ending it as a babysitter. I'm too old for this shit."

"What are you mumbling about, Mr. Pratt?" the colonel called out to him.

"Nothing, colonel, nothing at all," Pratt lied.

"It didn't look like nothing," the colonel said, smiling, and let the matter drop.

Clint was fast asleep in his bedroll when Mr. Pratt kicked his foot. "It's your watch, Clint," Mr. Pratt said, handing him a cup of coffee.

"Yes, sir," Clint responded as he sat up and took the coffee. He had been sleeping in his clothes, so all he had to do was put on his hat.

"Now, all you need to do is walk around the temporary pen that the remuda is in, and keep 'em calm. Just your presence there will deter any thieves or wild animals. Got that?"

"Wild animals?" Clint inquired.

"Yes, Clint, we are in the wild. And in the wild, there are wild animals," Mr. Pratt informed him.

"Yes, sir," he answered, then asked, "What kind of wild animals?" Mr. Pratt just walked away, shaking his head.

Clint had been on watch for about thirty minutes when he was spooked by dozens of night noises, the likes of which he'd never heard on the farm. He did his best to keep from panicking. He heard a twig snap behind him, and he nearly jumped out of his boots. He drew his pistol and turned to face what he thought would be a bear or a mountain lion, but it was only Dusty.

"Whoa now, son. Don't shoot me!" Dusty exclaimed.

"Oh, gosh, I'm sorry. I thought you were a bear," Clint blurted out as he stuffed the pistol back in his holster.

"So, how are you doing, young man?" Dusty asked, though he knew it wasn't going well.

"Just fine, Dusty," Clint put on a brave face, "except, I keep, ah, I keep..."

"You keep what, boy?" Dusty could see that Clint was scared.

"I keep hearing things… noises," Clint said.

"Oh, my."

"What?"

"It's probably jackalopes," Dusty said, looking around as if he was concerned about the critter he'd just mentioned.

"Jackalopes? What's a jackalope?" Clint asked, concern clearly showing in his face.

"They're half antelope and half jack rabbit," Dusty explained.

"There ain't no such thing!" Clint retorted, trying to reassure himself in the process.

"Oh, yes, there is," Dusty whispered. "They're the fiercest creature there is. Been known to tear a man's innards out. They're formed during lightning storms. Gets the critters all worked up, and they start fornicating amongst themselves." Dusty was going all out, and Clint started imagining all kinds of mixed up creatures. Just at that moment, the colonel appeared.

"Well, now, seems like I'm not the only one concerned about our greenhorn. How are you, Dusty?" the colonel asked.

"Just fine, Colonel. Seems Clint here is hearing noises. I told him all about the jackalopes and how dangerous they are and all." The colonel smiled at Dusty.

"You all have a wonderful night now," Dusty said as he walked away, grinning. Clint turned to the colonel to get answers.

"Is that true, Colonel? About the jackalopes and all?" Clint asked, clearly disturbed by the story Dusty was spinning.

The colonel smiled as he answered, "No, Clint, he was just pulling your leg."

"Now why would he go and do a thing like that?"

"Because he likes you. If he likes you, he'll pick on you. Now, you're doing just fine. Don't worry about those noises. You'll get used to them. We haven't seen any bear or mountain lions ever on the trail. Jackalopes. What a hoot," the colonel said, shaking his head as he walked away.

CHAPTER EIGHT

Every morning, the cowboys came to get their mount for the day. This morning, one cowboy grabbed Clint's personal horse from the herd.

"That's my horse. I'm afraid you can't have that one," Clint called out.

"All of them belong to the colonel, boy. I'll ride the one I want."

"No, sir, he belongs to me," Clint protested.

"And I just told you, I ride what I want," the cowpoke said defiantly. Lightning fast, Clint drew one of his weapons and had it pointed at the man. The cowboy stood there, frozen in fear.

"That's my horse. Now let him go," Clint snarled at him, slowly and deliberately.

"Put that away, Clint. Now!" Mr. Pratt shouted as he ran up. He and the colonel had been watching the entire time.

"He's trying to take my horse," Clint said, without lowering his gun or taking his eyes off the cowpoke.

"Get another horse," Mr. Pratt instructed the cowpoke. When he took the saddle off Clint's horse, Clint finally put his gun away. As the cowpoke started to saddle another horse, Mr. Pratt turned to Clint.

"I understand that's your horse, but we don't need to be pulling our weapons on each other. We need every man we've got to get this herd to Fort McPherson. Understood?" Mr. Pratt barked at Clint.

"Yes, sir," Clint said, sheepishly. "It's just—"

"It's just… nothing! If you pull your gun on a fellow cowpoke on this drive, you're out of here," Mr. Pratt snarled. "Now, go on about your job!" he said, dismissing Clint.

Mr. Pratt walked over to the cowpoke. "I expect you to listen to the wrangler when he tells you something about the horses. He was more than clear when he said the horse was his, and it is. So don't mess with that horse again."

"He's a damn kid. A greenhorn, and I don't take no orders from a greenhorn," the man replied. Without warning, Pratt lunged at the man, slamming him into the horse he had just saddled, knocking him to the ground. Mr. Pratt then stood over him, his hand on his gun. "I gave you an order, mister, and if you can't—or won't—follow that order, you can leave right now," Pratt angrily told him.

"Okay, okay. I'll leave his horse alone," the cowpoke said.

"If I see or hear about you giving that boy a hard time, or you're messing with his horse, you'll have me to answer to, and believe me, you won't like what happens to you," Pratt threatened. "Now, get to work!"

"Yes, sir," the cowpoke said as he stood, mounted his horse, and rode out into the herd.

"You were a little rough on him, weren't you?" the colonel asked when Pratt rejoined him.

"You said you wanted me to look after the kid, didn't you?" Pratt countered.

"Yeah, but putting the fear of God in the man?" the colonel questioned.

"That cowpoke is a hothead, and if he thinks he can deal with Clint on his terms, he'd be pulling a gun on Clint some time when I'm not looking," Pratt explained.

"Did you see how fast Clint drew that gun?" the colonel asked Pratt.

"Yeah, I did. You're going to have teach him some self-control or he's going to get himself killed. He'll either meet someone faster than him or get hung or murdered," Pratt shared.

"He's the fastest I've ever seen," the colonel mused.

"Yeah, but there's always someone faster. On any given day, anyone can kill anyone else."

"I think I'll have a word or two with him," the colonel said as they rode off to check the herd.

Riding along the trail, they passed through a variety of terrain, from flat prairies to rolling hills to mountains. The days ran into one another, just daylight and night. Clint had lost track of which day it actually was by the time they finally arrived at the fort to deliver the herd. After the herd was tucked away into the holding pens, the colonel took Clint aside.

"Clint, I need to pay the rest of the men, but I'd like to speak to you personally. Do you mind sticking around for a while?" he asked. Clint was unsure why the colonel needed to speak with him, but he didn't have anywhere to go.

"Sure, Colonel," he replied. "No problem."

"Good. See you in a bit. Here's your money. I already took out your part of the room in Sedalia," the colonel said, handing Clint an envelope. Clint quickly emptied it and placed the money in his pocket.

"Thanks, Colonel," Clint replied.

"Clint, you've ruined your life by becoming a cowboy! You can't get much lower!" Clint heard someone talking behind him and turned around to see Mr. Pratt.

"Mr. Pratt! I got paid!" Clint exclaimed, taking one of the gold coins out of his pocket and holding it out in his hand.

"Don't spend it all in one place, boy! Hey, as a matter of fact, you want to join me? Let's go get us a bath and a good meal over at the hotel," Mr. Pratt suggested.

"You know, that sounds good," Clint replied.

As the two men were enjoying their bath, the colonel came in.

"I see you boys are getting the grime off. Clint, how do you feel after your first drive?" asked the colonel.

"I feel great, Colonel! When can I do it again?" Clint asked enthusiastically. The colonel looked at Mr. Pratt, then back at Clint.

"May I speak freely in front of Mr. Pratt, Clint?" the colonel asked. Clint looked at Mr. Pratt, then back at the colonel. He wasn't sure where this was heading, but he shrugged his shoulders.

"Sure, Colonel. I don't have any secrets from him," Clint answered, though his face said he wasn't sure what to make of the situation.

"Well, you see, Clint, my next drive isn't until spring."

"Oh," Clint said, looking sad. It was obvious he was disappointed. The colonel and Mr. Pratt looked at each other for a moment.

 "Clint," the colonel said, "cowboys are men who never grow up. For some, it's just a phase they go through. For others, it's a lifestyle. Now, I normally pay the men and they go on their way. They drift from here to there picking up work where they can. I don't see you doing that, Clint. And from what you told me, I don't suspect you have any desire to go home."

"No, sir. I sure don't," Clint confirmed.

"Well, then, here's my offer. You return to the ranch with me, Mr. Pratt, Dusty, and Cole. I could use a good horse wrangler, and I've seen that you can do that. But there's a condition," the colonel said, waiting for Clint to react. Clint looking up at him expectantly. "You let me educate you. That means book learning. I've got enough dumb cowboys on the ranch," the colonel explained.

"I ain't never had much book learning before," Clint told him.

"You've never had," the colonel corrected him.

"What?" Clint asked, confused.

"The proper way to say it is: I've never had any book learning. Your education starts now, provided you accept my offer," the colonel said.

"I've never had any book learning, but I'm willing," Clint replied, a smile on his face.

"Good. Now, you men finish getting cleaned up and meet me for dinner in an hour. It's on me," the colonel stated.

"Sounds good to me! What do you say, Clint?" Mr. Pratt asked.

"Yes, sir! I mean, sure, Mr. Pratt," Clint stumbled through the reply.

"Good. I'll see you then," the colonel said. With that, he stood up and left.

When he was sure the colonel was out of earshot, Mr. Pratt leaned over towards Clint.
"There's something you should know about the colonel."

"What is it?" Clint asked.

Mr. Pratt hesitated for a moment and then, speaking softly, began to share his secret.

"The colonel was married once and had a son. His son defied him and entered the war when he was about your age, maybe a little older, but not by more than a couple years. After he left, the colonel would stand on his porch every evening waiting for his return, but he never saw him again. He's been trying ever since to replace him, and he's been disappointed time and again. He's getting old, and he's feeling a bit lost. He wants to have someone he can be proud of, someone he can leave his ranch to. I just want to caution you not to disappoint him. If you don't think you can follow through, don't take his offer. I mean it, Clint. I think of him as a brother, and I'll treat you like my own son should you follow through. But, if you disappoint him by failing to follow through and do your best to learn, you'll have me to deal with, and I ain't no washed up cowpoke." Mr. Pratt gave Clint a hard look. Clint felt a shiver run up his spine.

"I won't let you all down, Mr. Pratt. I promise," Clint replied, after taking a minute to think about it.

"I know you won't, son. Now, let's finish up and go have that dinner," Mr. Pratt said, a smile on his face.

On the way to the dining hall, Clint and Pratt passed the saloon. They saw Cole busy gambling and drinking hard with a couple of the men from the drive, including the cowpoke who had tried to ride Clint's horse.

"Well, if it isn't the greenhorn babe in the woods," the cowpoke slurred as he stood up and stepped clear of the table so he had a clear line of sight between him and Clint. Clint looked around quickly. Mr. Pratt had gone to the front desk, and Clint was alone with a drunk cowpoke threatening him.

"Pratt isn't there, little boy. It's just me and you. You were quick to pull your gun on me when I had my hands full of saddle. What say you try it again, now that I can defend myself?" the cowpoke snarled.

"I don't want to fight you. I apologize for acting like a fool out there on the range," Clint said, trying to defuse the situation. "Let me buy you a drink, and we can bury the hatchet."

The only thing we're going to bury, greenhorn, is you!" the cowpoke shouted. The room got deathly quiet. The man grabbed for his gun, but he had drunk so much his reflexes were dulled and slow, compared to a sober young buck with tons of natural talent and solid, practiced skills.

Clint reacted just as his pappy had taught him. As soon as the cowpoke made his move, Clint drew his gun, lightning quick, and fired before the cowpoke could clear his holster. Clint watched in fascination as the cowpoke slowly slumped to the floor, then fell forward, dead.

The colonel heard the shot and raced from the dining room to the saloon. Mr. Pratt ran to Clint's side.

"What happened?" Mr. Pratt demanded.

"He threatened me, and then drew his gun," Clint mumbled weakly. He'd never killed a man before.

"But I told you to avoid him!" Pratt said as the colonel entered the room.

"What happened?" the colonel shouted as he looked at the man on the floor and at Clint holding his gun. "Mr. Pratt, what happened?" the colonel asked again.

"I don't know. I was at the front desk," Mr. Pratt answered.

"I told you to look out for him," the colonel snarled.

It was then that Cole stood up and walked over to the colonel and Mr. Pratt. "Colonel, I saw the whole thing. Clint didn't do anything to cause this. Hobart there has had a grudge against him since the day they argued over the horse. I heard him say he'd get Clint after the drive when Mr. Pratt wasn't around. Clint and Mr. Pratt came in, and then Mr. Pratt stepped out. Hobart jumped up and began threatening Clint. Clint tried to buy him a drink, and he even apologized, but Hobart wouldn't have it. He started to draw first, but Clint here was just way too fast. He drew and shot Hobart before Hobart could even get his gun out of his holster. He shot him in self-defense," said Cole.

"Thank you, Cole," the colonel said, turning to Clint. "Are you okay?" he asked.

"I guess so. I don't rightly know what I feel. I tried to reason with him. I even apologized. But he wouldn't hear of it. He started to draw on me, and I just reacted like my pappy taught me," Clint replied.

"It's okay, son. Some men just push things," the colonel told him. "It wasn't your fault. It was self- defense."

"But I killed him. I didn't want to kill him, but I wasn't going to let him kill me," Clint told the colonel and Mr. Pratt.

"I'll handle the sheriff," Mr. Pratt offered, and the colonel nodded as he led Clint out of the saloon.

"Put your gun away," the colonel said as they left the saloon. "I was going to have this talk with you back at the ranch, but I figure I'd better have it now before things spiral out of control."

"I'm sorry," Clint told the colonel, "I'm not a killer, but my pappy told me to never let anyone kill me. That was why he gave me his guns and taught me how to use them."

"I know. It was a good thing he did teach you. He did an excellent job, but you don't want to become known as a fast draw or a gunfighter. You'll become a target, and sooner or later, you'll face someone faster than you. It's more than likely it'll be sooner rather than later. Never brag that you're fast, or faster than most, because men will want to test you. Always do your best to avoid becoming entangled with men who are looking for trouble. You'll know them by the way they carry themselves. I'll do my best to teach you how to spot troublemakers and how to disarm them without having to risk a gunfight," the colonel advised. "Now, put this whole incident out of your mind, and let's go have a good meal. Have you taken a room in the hotel for tonight?" the colonel asked.

"Ah… no, I hadn't thought about it," Clint replied absently.

"Don't sweat it. I'll take care of it."

They sat down at the table for dinner. Clint leaned towards the colonel and began talking. "I don't want to disappoint you, Colonel. I want to grow up to be a good man. A man with a future and in good standing with his neighbors. But that cowpoke, he was drunk and started to draw on me. I had no choice. It was either him or me," Clint said as tears welled up in his eyes.

The colonel handed him his napkin and rested his hand on his shoulder. "I'm here to help you reach those goals, Clint. I won't let you down," he said. Dinner was a silent affair as Clint, Mr. Pratt, and the colonel ate in a hurry, then headed up to bed. At first light, they were on the trail for the colonel's ranch in Texas. The colonel led them, followed by Mr. Pratt, Dusty, Clint, and a hungover Cole bringing up the rear.

CHAPTER NINE

They rode until the landscape became lush with grass, with hundreds of head of cattle and calves. They stopped on a ridge and looked down.

"Well, there it is, Clint. Your new home. A slice of heaven," the colonel said as the five of them looked down from the ridgetop at the huge range that the colonel owned.

"Sure is pretty," Clint answered.

Clint was looking down on the biggest spread he had ever seen. Smack dab in the middle of it was a sprawling ranch-style house surrounded by cottonwoods. It was flanked by a stable, a bunkhouse, a single standing cottage, and several other outbuildings.

As they rode down to the house, Clint laid eyes on her for the first time. She was standing on the front porch in a sheer white dress. Clint could see the outline of her body. *This must be heaven*, he thought, *because I'm looking at an angel.*

"About time you showed up. I was getting worried, until I received that telegram," the girl admonished the colonel. She looked intently at Clint, then asked, "Who do we have here? Where did you pick up this stray?" She studied him from his hat to his boots, not sure if it was his good looks or innocence that was making her breathless.

"This is Clint Cain, our new wrangler. This here is my niece, Amber Lynn," the colonel said.

Amber Lynn was a couple of years older than Clint. She had lost both parents in the war, so the colonel had taken her in and raised her as his own. She was only seventeen but had seen more than some women twice her age. Her eyes were big and round, and as blue as the big Texas sky. Her hair was as golden as the winter grass, with a hint of dew in it. Her lips were full. When she smiled, Clint's heart skipped a beat. He felt lightheaded. She was simply the most beautiful girl Clint had ever seen. She also seemed the most unapproachable creature imaginable.

"It sure is good to be back," Dusty said, stepping down from the wagon and walking over to Amber Lynn. He gave her a big hug.

"Boys," Pratt said, "you know the routine. You take care of the horses, Cole. Clint, you help him. Dusty—"

"Yeah, I know," Dusty interrupted him. "Pack away the chuck wagon and its gear. Been there, done that," he stated as he headed back to the wagon.

"We're having a coming home dinner tonight, men. Six sharp. Be here and dress appropriately," the colonel told them.

Clint and Cole took the horses and headed for the barn. Mr. Pratt headed to his cabin, and Dusty headed for a small building off to the side of the corral.

"Did you see her?" Cole asked Clint as they walked towards the stables.

"A blind man would have seen her," Clint offered.

"I'm gonna have her someday. Every inch of her. I'm gonna have her and Mr. Pratt's job." The way Cole was talking, Clint was getting a little nervous.

"You shouldn't talk about a woman like that," Clint told him.

"Really?" Cole said, looking at Clint. "What do you know about women?"

Clint thought for a moment, then said, "Well, I, ah... I know they're all females." Cole burst out laughing.

That evening, Clint was awestruck as he entered the colonel's house for the first time. His eyes widened as he walked into the foyer. He had never seen the likes of a home like this. All his life he had been used to sparse accommodation. To his left was a living room. He stood there and admired the handsomely furnished interior. There were plush carpets, inlaid tables, an ornate fireplace, a velvet sofa, and upholstered chairs. The one thing that stood out for Clint were the books in the library to his right. Shelves and shelves of books. He had no idea that that many books even existed.

"Need an escort?" The voice startled Clint. It was Amber Lynn. She had come up behind him, and he turned and looked at her. He couldn't help but stare. *God, she's gorgeous.* He didn't know what to say. "Well, cat got your tongue?" she asked.

"Ah... er... ah... no," Clint stumbled. He stood there, feeling awkward.

"Okay, cowboy, here's how it works. Raise your right arm," she said. Clint stuck his arm straight out. "No, dummy, like this," she said, putting his arm back down. "Now, make your hand into a fist. Good. Now, place your hand right there, just below your ribcage... there. Now, I hook my arm into yours, and away we go," Amber Lynn smiled as she tugged his arm, leading the way.

"Where are we going?" Clint asked.

"Why, to the dining room, silly."

"Like at a hotel?" Clint asked.

Amber Lynn grinned. "Sort of." A moment later, they stepped into the dining room, arm-in-arm.

"Well, look who's here!" the colonel said.

Clint took her to her chair and pulled it out for her. He started to walk away, but Amber Lynn grabbed him by his arm. "You sit here, Clint, beside me."

At the head of the table sat the colonel, joined by Mr. Pratt on his right and Dusty on his left. Seated along the sides of the long table were four men Clint hadn't met yet. There was no Cole. The colonel stood as soon as Clint was seated and started speaking.

"First, I want to thank the men who kept up the ranch while we were gone," the colonel offered.

"I had something to do with that!" Amber Lynn said, emphatically.

"Yes, and thank you, too, Amber Lynn." The colonel continued, "I pray that we are all blessed, healthy, and happy this evening."

"Hear, hear!" everyone at the table replied.

"Now, Clint, since you're the new member of the group, would you mind saying grace?" the colonel asked as he took his seat. Clint swallowed hard. He had never said grace before and had never spoken in front of such a large group.

"I don't know… I've never…" he stammered, when Amber Lynn spoke up.

"Oh, go ahead, Clint," she said as she poked him in the ribs, trying to encourage him. "You can't be any worse at it than I am."

"The only prayer I know is the one I've heard my pappy say. He told me that he learned it during the war," Clint offered as he looked at the colonel for approval.

"Well, let's hear it. Come on," the colonel said, and Amber Lynn smiled at him.

"Okay, here goes," Clint started, and everyone bowed their heads. Clint bowed his like the others and closed his eyes. "Good bread. Good meat. Damn, let's eat. Amen," Clint prayed. When he raised his head, everyone was staring at him. Then they all burst out in laughter, with Clint joining in. He was now officially part of the family.

CHAPTER TEN

The years passed, and Clint grew intellectually and physically. He had tried to absorb everything he had seen and been taught. He had learned the tools needed to be a cowboy and a gentleman. The colonel educated him, alongside Amber Lynn, who had become his mentor. Under their guidance, it didn't take long for Clint to catch up on his lost years of education. He thought he might become a lawyer someday.

He learned everything he needed to know from Mr. Pratt about how to work a ranch and drive cattle. He went on every drive and displayed his courage and skills numerous times. He had matured into a confident and handsome young man. He was five feet ten inches tall and well-built at one hundred and sixty pounds. He had a nose like a Greek god, a sensuous mouth, and sharp eyes. He sported a pencil-thin mustache that went past his lower lip, complemented with a soul patch. He knew who he was and where he was going.

The colonel had sculpted him into a southern gentleman. He had become everything the colonel wanted him to be, and Clint liked the feeling. He also enjoyed the feeling of being with Amber Lynn. They had grown up together, and their relationship had matured. There was no doubt in anyone's mind that they cared for each other. For Clint, Amber Lynn was the most desirable woman on earth. For Amber Lynn, Clint was so handsome he was almost beautiful, and he had a heart to match.

Cole, as well, had grown and matured into the consummate cowboy. He also had a deep, unbridled hatred for Clint. It infuriated him that the colonel—hell, the entire ranch—treated Clint like the chosen one. He had also seen the way Amber Lynn doted over Clint. He had stood by long enough.

Cole had heard a secret, through closed doors, that his time was coming. Mr. Pratt was getting long in the tooth and wasn't up to driving cattle anymore. Tonight, the colonel was holding a dinner dance for all his business associates and friends. He was going to make an announcement that would change everyone's world. Cole was sure his destiny was about to be fulfilled. He had done all he was asked, and he deserved to become the new foreman. Or at least he thought he did.

Clint had seen a lot of things on the trail these last five years that would frighten the average man. Tornados, stampedes, wild Indians, and he had faced it all. But the thought of what he would have to confront tonight scared him to death—dancing.

He had tried square dancing back in Missouri, but he had never taken to it as he always felt a bit out of place. He kept reminding himself what Mr. Pratt had told him when he was breaking horses. "No balls, no glory." If a horse throws you off, get right back on. But what if he forgot the steps the colonel had taught him in private? That was his biggest worry. To try to ensure he didn't, he had purposely waited for Cole, Dusty, and the others to leave the bunkhouse so he could practice one more time. He felt like a fool dancing about the bunkhouse by himself, but when he finished, he felt he'd do okay. He still prayed for God to help him, just the same. He checked his suit in the mirror one last time and repeated again what Mr. Pratt had said: "No balls, no glory."

Amber Lynn stood in front of the full-length mirror checking every seam, every crease in her dress, straightening the pleats, over and over again. God, she was nervous. She had rearranged her hair a dozen times. Up? Down? Bow? No bow? Ribbons? Pearls? Bracelets? Oh, what the hell. Half the cowboys out there wouldn't care if she was wearing a flour sack and was bald. But it wasn't half the cowboys that she wanted to notice her. She had only one in mind. The one who she wanted to dance with. The one who would tell her she was beautiful.

The dining room had turned into a ballroom. A band was playing lively music, and the room was filled. It was standing room only. The moment Clint entered the room, he saw Amber Lynn. She was on the other side and was by far the prettiest woman there. He strolled boldly through the crowd, took her hand, and led her onto the dance floor. He had to get this out of the way before he lost his nerve. He was agile, almost light on his feet. Amber Lynn immediately recognized the moves as her uncle's. She cut her eyes towards him. The colonel nodded to acknowledge her. He knew she knew. She smiled back.

"You look beautiful tonight," Clint whispered in her ear.

"I knew you'd say that," she replied with a smile. She looked up at Clint and became enraptured. Her body tingled, and her skin prickled. She was in heaven.

Cole, who had been watching the entire scene, rose to his feet. He walked straight towards the dancing couple. Amber Lynn saw him coming, and the way she looked at him gave him pause. But he had drunk enough to pluck up his courage, so he continued on his mission.

"May I cut in?" he asked and pushed Clint back without his permission.

Clint was not happy, but being the gentleman he was, he yielded. Amber Lynn could smell the liquor on Cole's breath and feel the sweatiness of his hands. She was repulsed by Cole. The song ended, and she quickly turned towards Clint, the only man she had eyes for. Cole fumed with jealousy.

"Clint, would you escort me outside? I need some fresh air."

"Certainly," Clint said.

They strolled away from the house. In the half-darkness, the moon was beginning to rise. Clint wrapped his arms around Amber Lynn from behind. He ran his hand past the hem of her bodice, and for the first time, he held her delicate breast. She gasped but did not resist. They had not seen the looming shadow in the darkness that was Cole.

"Well, well. What do we have here?" Cole said. "Two lovebirds in the moonlight."

"What do you want, Cole?" Clint asked as he turned to face him.

"What do I want? Let's see, what do I want? Oh, my friend, Clint. It's not what I want. It's what I'm gonna get," Cole snarled as he stepped closer.

"You're drunk, Cole. I suggest you go back inside," Clint told him.

"And what? Miss the show?" Cole slurred as he grabbed Amber Lynn's hand. She resisted.

"Let me go!" she spat at Cole.

I've got enough love for both of us," Cole said, squeezing her hand tighter.

"I'm warning you, Cole!" Clint told him.

"Let me go, I said!" Amber Lynn yelled. She slapped Cole hard across the face as he tried to pull her closer.

"You asked for it!" Clint said and charged Cole.

Clint delivered a left cross to Cole's jaw, knocking him into the bushes behind him. He lay there, not moving at first, then sat up. He rubbed his face and looked at Clint, his face a mask of hatred.

"You're gonna be sorry you did that. Real sorry, and real soon," Cole snarled.

Clint ignored Cole, took Amber Lynn's hand, and started back towards the ranch house. They went inside, mingling with the crowd for a few minutes, exchanging pleasantries. Mr. Pratt came up to them.

"The colonel would like to see you in his office, Clint," he said firmly.

"Yes, sir. If you'll excuse me, Amber Lynn," Clint said. Amber Lynn looked confused and worried.

Clint and Mr. Pratt entered the colonel's office. He was sitting behind his desk but stood when they entered.

"Clint. Glad to see you. Are you having a good time at the party?"

"Yes, Colonel," Clint answered, unsure what he was really asking.

"I have some news I want to share with you," the colonel told him. Clint felt himself tense. The colonel looked over at Mr. Pratt. A few seconds seemed like minutes to Clint.

"Well?" Mr. Pratt said. "Are you going to tell him or shall I?" The colonel smiled and began to speak.

"Clint, Mr. Pratt here has decided to retire. That means we're going to need a new foreman." Clint's jaw dropped. The colonel continued, "I had a choice between you and Cole. It's no secret that Cole has always coveted the job, but I need a man who is going to put the interests of the ranch above his own. An intelligent man, a man of honor. After conferring with Mr. Pratt, the choice was quite simple. Congratulations, Clint, you're our new foreman!"

Clint looked at Mr. Pratt, then back at the colonel, not sure what to say.

"Well, son, are you going to say anything? Or just stand there with your mouth open until your teeth die from exposure?" Mr. Pratt asked. Clint grabbed the colonel's hand and began to shake it furiously. Then he did the same with Mr. Pratt.

"Thank you, Mr. Pratt! Thank you, Colonel!"

"Don't thank me yet, son. You might curse me before this is all over," the colonel said. "Let's have a drink to celebrate," he added.

"You talked me into it," said Mr. Pratt. Clint didn't argue, gratefully accepting the drink and the job.

The colonel poured three shots of fine whiskey. "Here's to the future of the Billups ranch," the colonel said as he raised his glass. Mr. Pratt and Clint raised theirs.

"To the ranch!" they said in unison as they downed their drinks.

"Well, let's go make the announcement," the colonel said, placing his glass down on his desk.

"What about Cole? He's going to be livid," Mr. Pratt asked.

"He'll have to get over it. My ranch, my choice," the colonel answered. "Now, let's go."

The three men re-entered the party. Clint walked over to Amber Lynn and stood beside her.

"What did he want?" she asked, with a wrinkled brow.

"You'll find out in a minute," he said, smiling at her.

"Ladies and gentlemen! May I have your attention, please," the colonel said. Clint looked around and saw Cole, standing just ten feet from the colonel, grinning from ear to ear. "My friend and foreman, Mr. Pratt, has an announcement to make!" The crowd hushed and everyone turned towards Mr.

Pratt, who was standing on the other side of the colonel from Cole.

"Well, I'm not a man of many words," Mr. Pratt said, "so I'm just going to come out and say it. I'm retiring." There was a faint moan heard in the room.

"Well, not completely," he added. "See, I did manage to save a little poke at this lousy job, and I bought a saloon a few miles from here." The crowd laughed.

"Where he'll drink up all the profits!" the colonel joked. The crowd laughed again.

"Now, don't you all fret. I have an announcement to make also," the colonel continued. "Seeing how Mr. Pratt is leaving us, I need a replacement. Now it wasn't easy, but I believe I've chosen the right man for the job." Cole looked as though he was about to burst. He just knew he was going to hear his name and even took a couple steps towards the colonel.

"I've chosen Clint Cain! Come on up here, Clint!" the colonel said, gesturing to Clint. Amber Lynn looked at Clint. He looked back and winked.

"Now just wait a damn minute!" Cole bellowed, storming towards the colonel. "I'm the best man for the job! I'm a better cowboy than he'll ever be!" Cole spat. The crowd was shocked by his outburst.

"Cole!" Mr. Pratt barked.

"Wait, just wait, Mr. Pratt. Let him have his say," the colonel interrupted.

"I was here way before him, and I've shown my ability to run this place! I deserve to be the new foreman!" Cole stated stubbornly.

"Are you done?" the colonel asked politely. Cole looked at the colonel, fuming, as the colonel continued. "To begin with, Cole, yes, you have been here longer, and I have offered you the same opportunities that I offered Clint. The difference is, Clint took advantage of those opportunities whereas you didn't," the colonel stated.

"Oh, he took advantage of them all right, if you're talking about your niece, Colonel! Yeah! He sure did!"

"Now just one minute there, Cole!" Clint bellowed, stepping forward. The colonel placed his hand on Clint's chest to hold him back.

"I've got this, Clint," the colonel said. "Cole, I've given you every opportunity to better yourself since you've been here, but you've behaved like some spoiled brat, doing nothing but chasing women, drinking, and raising hell. That's not the kind of man I want to handle my affairs. Considering your past conduct and your outburst tonight, Cole, you're fired."

"You'll regret this!" Cole said, looking at Clint, Mr. Pratt, and the colonel. "Yes, sir! You're going to regret this!" He turned and walked through the crowd, pushing people out of his way as he went, and headed out the door.

"I apologize for the scene you've just had to witness, my friends. Please continue. Don't let this spoil your fun," the colonel said as the partygoers surrounded Clint and Mr. Pratt to congratulate them.

CHAPTER ELEVEN

It was an emotional and exciting time at the ranch. Mr. Pratt had his belongings loaded onto the wagon, and when he was ready to go, everyone gathered around to bid him farewell.

"You know you're welcome back here anytime, old man," the colonel told Mr. Pratt.

"I appreciate that. You know, too, if you ever make it out my way, the first drink is on me. After that, you pay like everyone else." They smiled at each other. Then Mr. Pratt turned to Clint.

"Clint, I've known quite a few cowboys who weren't very good men, and I've known a lot of good men who weren't very good cowboys. You, on the other hand, are a good man, and a good cowboy," he said, pausing for a minute before continuing, "You look after the colonel, and especially that little lady."

"Oh, he will. I'll see to that," Amber Lynn said as she walked up with a tear in her eye.

"Dusty, I'm going to miss those special biscuits you make on the trail," Pratt shouted, even though Pratt hadn't seen the trail in five years. His trail lately was confined to the rocking chair on the front porch of his cabin over by the corral.

"You mean those special ones I make for Clint?" Dusty asked, and the men laughed.

"Enough of this. Let me get out of here before I change my mind," Mr. Pratt said, a tear slowly rolling from the corner of his eye. He turned, quickly climbed aboard the wagon, then pulled away as everyone waved goodbye.

"Well, Mr. Cain, are you ready to take over the reins?" the colonel asked, turning to Clint.

"Ready as I'll ever be," Clint said with a smile.

Clint was moved into the cabin once occupied by Mr. Pratt. It was a far cry better than the bunkhouse he shared with the other men. He didn't have to listen to any more snoring or farting. He was squaring away his things when Amber Lynn walked in.

"So, how does it feel?" she asked.

"How does what feel?"

"To be in charge. Have all the weight upon your shoulders?"

"You sure do have a way of making it easier," he said. "In fact, you've made my whole life better."
She chuckled.

"I'm proud of you, Clint. My uncle trusts you and believes in you. So do I."

"I won't let him down," Clint replied.

"I know you won't. Are you afraid you might?" she asked.

"Afraid? No, not afraid. Concerned would be a better word."

"There's something else you should be concerned about," she said cryptically.

"As if I don't have enough on my plate. What else?" he asked.

"You'll see," she said, turning towards the door. She looked over her shoulder and gave him a smile.

That night, as Clint lay in bed, a million thoughts ran through his head. He tossed and turned. He was so occupied in thought, he didn't hear the door open nor the footsteps across the floor. He didn't see the shadow float across the wall.

"Clint?" He thought he heard a voice and turned over to see Amber Lynn standing beside his bed. He could see the silhouette of her body through her thin nightgown. Without a word, he pulled the covers back, inviting her in. She slid in beside him and took him between her legs, shifting to make room for him. She tried to speak but couldn't find the words. They touched each other in places that had never been touched. It brought them both pleasure and sealed their bond.

"What do I... I've never... I don't know how…" Amber said.

"I know, sweetheart. Neither do I," he whispered. Her confusion disappeared as Clint placed his lips upon her nipple. She moaned in pleasure. She could resist no more. Her hand found him, and she allowed him to join her. He entered her in one smooth stroke. Her body tensed, and she grabbed the pillow and bit it. Her raging need overcame her discomfort, and she began to match his movement. Like dancers, they moved as one. Joy enveloped them as their eyes met. They drew each other in as their bodies tightened. They couldn't have fit better together. They lifted each other into thin air and then drifted back to earth, both unwilling to land. They lost their innocence and gave each other their hearts.

"Oh, my God!" Amber said as she looked out the window at the first rays of the morning sun. Clint was startled awake and rolled over, enveloping her in his arms.

"What time is it?" she wanted to know.

"I don't know. Almost morning," Clint answered, still half asleep.

"I've got to get back to the house," she said, pushing him away. "If my uncle finds me gone, he'll have a fit." She got up and pulled on her heavy robe, leaving her nightgown on the floor by the bed.

"If he catches you, I'll tell him it was all your idea," Clint said, jokingly.

"You would. If I didn't love you, I'd hate you," she said mockingly as she went out the door.

"I love you, too," he called out to her back.

A couple months later, Clint knocked upon the colonel's door.

"Come in," the colonel answered, and Clint strode in with his hat in his hand.

"Sir... Colonel... I have a question to ah... ah..."

"What's wrong, Clint? You seem more nervous than a cat in a room full of rocking chairs," the colonel said.

"May I sit down?" Clint asked.

"Sure. Go ahead. It's not about the upcoming drive, is it? You'll do just fine," the colonel assured him.

"Oh, no, sir. I'm looking forward to it. It's more important than that," Clint said.

"Well, go ahead. Spit it out," the colonel told him.

Clint took a deep breath. "I know when I came here, I was nothing more than a young, ignorant, dirt farmer's son. You took me in, and you and Mr. Pratt literally taught me everything I know and have given me everything I have. Without you, I don't know where I would be in life right now. Probably dead, shot down in some gunfight. I've never asked for anything, well, until now," Clint said.

"Go on."

"I wish to ask you for Amber Lynn's hand in marriage," Clint blurted, then sat there staring at the floor. The colonel sat there for a few seconds, then he rose to his feet. He turned, walked to the window, and looked out as if he were looking into the past.

"I was married once as you know. Her name was Anne. I lost her when my son was born. Before she died, she took off her engagement ring. I begged her not to, but she insisted. She told me that she loved me so much, she wanted me to find someone else worthy of me." He turned around and opened a drawer to his desk. He took out a silver box and opened it. In it was that same beautiful engagement ring. "I want you to give this to Amber Lynn," the colonel said.

"Colonel, I couldn't. I mean—"

"Clint, I couldn't think of a man worthier of Amber Lynn's love. You've done everything I've asked of you and more. Now take it. You have my blessing."

"Thank you, Colonel," Clint gushed.

"Don't thank me yet, son. You might curse me before this is over." They looked at each other and began to laugh. The line had become their private joke over the years.

Amber Lynn could feel the life inside her. She knew she was pregnant long before her flow had stopped. She couldn't feel it physically, but she knew it was there. Two heartbeats. Hers, and the one she and Clint had made through their lovemaking. She had to tell Clint before he left. God forbid something were to happen to him on the trail, and he didn't know he was going to be a father. She waited for him at his cabin.

Clint bolted from the colonel's office, looking for Amber Lynn. He had to ask her and ask her now. He found her standing on the porch of his cabin, a solemn look on her face.

"What's wrong?" Clint asked as he saw tears beginning to well up in her eyes.

"I have something to tell you," she said, fighting back the tears.

"Well, I have something to ask you. May I go first?" Clint asked.

"Sure," she said halfheartedly.

Clint stepped on the porch, got down on one knee, took out the silver box the colonel had given him and opened it. Amber Lynn recognized it and immediately felt the breath leave her body.

"I know that I'm nothing more than a trail-worn cowboy. I don't know if I'll ever be anything more than that. All I know is, I want you to be my wife," Clint told her. Amber burst into tears as he slipped the ring on her finger. He stood and put his arms around her.

"I guess those tears mean yes?" he asked her. She nodded. "Now, what's your news?"

"We're going to have a baby," she said, half laughing, half crying, but smiling the whole time.

"We're going to have a baby?" Clint repeated as he held her at arm's length and looked her up and down. "Really!" he said, his face beaming. "This is my lucky day! I find out I'm going to be a husband and a father on the same day! Oh… How are we going to tell the colonel you're pregnant?" Clint asked next.

"Are you crazy? We're not. I'm no more than six or seven weeks at most. I can hide it until you return. Then we'll be married, and no one will be the wiser," she told him.

"Good idea," Clint thought, one less thing to worry about right now.

"I know. I'm the woman. We always have the good ideas," Amber pointed out, and they fell into each other's arms and kissed, deep and long.

The next day, Clint again found himself in the colonel's office. This time was at the colonel's request, just hours before he was to start the drive.

"Well, Clint, you're about to lead your first drive. How do you feel?" the colonel asked.

"Confident, Colonel. I've got this. I won't let you down," Clint told him, beaming.

"Confident enough to go it alone?"

"Alone? You mean, without you?" Clint asked, a look of concern on his face.

"Precisely. You see, Clint, something's come up. Something important that I have to stay behind and handle. There's a lot going on here that you need to know, now you're the new foreman. There's another rancher just outside my spread. His name is King Elks. Everybody calls him 'King,' and he acts like one at times. He owns half the town and is trying to take over the entire county. There's quite a few acres that are up for sale and if he gets them, his ranch will literally surround mine.

I intend on getting them first, and I know I can. But, if I go on this drive, I'll lose my chance. Now, I know that this drive is going all the way to Fort Lewis, Colorado. But you have the best handpicked cowboys, and Dusty will be with you. I know you can do this. It's at least a twenty-five-day drive, one way. You can handle it. I'm depending on you, son. We need that sale to finalize the purchase of those acres," the colonel said.

"Yes, sir. I won't let you down," Clint confirmed.

"Good. I knew I could count on you, son. As we'd planned, you pull out in the morning," the colonel reminded him.

"Will do, Colonel."

Son. He called me son, Clint thought as he left the office and then smiled.

The early morning dew was glistening as the sun was just breaking over the horizon. Clint was about to lead his first drive. The colonel and Amber Lynn were seeing him off.

"How will you miss me if you don't leave?" Amber Lynn asked.

"I guess you're right. The sooner I leave, the sooner I'll be back," Clint countered.

"Exactly. Now go get 'em, cowboy," she said as she turned her horse back to the ranch house. Clint smiled and got on his horse.

"See you when I return, Colonel," Clint said as he rode off after the herd.

"Good luck, Clint. Be safe. Take care of him, Dusty," the colonel called out to their backs.

Dusty called back, "I'm going to leave him for the jackalope!" The colonel chuckled and waved goodbye.

CHAPTER TWELVE

The sun was beginning to set. Amber Lynn was in the kitchen warming the evening meal while she awaited the return of her uncle. He had gone into town to take care of some business and would be arriving home shortly. She didn't hear the front door open or the footsteps down the hallway and across the floor as the figure crept up right behind her.

"Looky here. What do I see? If it ain't the little homemaker." She knew that voice—Cole. She spun around, and there he was not five feet away, with an evil grin on his face.

"How did you get in here, and what do you want?" she demanded.

"Now, is that any way to greet an old friend?" Cole hissed at her like the snake he was. It was obvious he'd been drinking.

"Get out now! My uncle will be back any minute!" she yelled at him, but he didn't move. He just continued to stand there, grinning wickedly at her.

"Oh, I hope he is. Got some business to conduct with him, too. But first, you. You see, Amber Lynn, I knew I was going to have you all along, one way or another. Way before Mr. Fancy Pants Clint ever arrived here," Cole told her. As he stepped closer, she grabbed a frying pan and lifted it up to hit him.

"Whoa, now, you going to hit me with that pan?" he asked as he slowly drew one of his pistols.

"Stay away from me! I swear… I'll…"

"You swear what?" he asked and lunged forward, trying to grab her arm with his free hand. At that precise moment, the colonel walked into the room with his gun drawn.

"Let her go, Cole," he shouted. Cole spun around, using Amber Lynn as a shield.

"Well, hello, Colonel. Glad you could join us," he said, pointing his weapon at the colonel.

"What do you want? Money? Gold? I've got both in the house. Let me get it for you. Just let her go," the colonel said, but Cole just chuckled—a sinister, maniacal chuckle.

"You think you can buy me off, after you ruined my life?" Cole snarled. "You ain't as smart as you claim oh-mister-high-and-mighty-southern-gentleman, Colonel."

"Then what is it that you want?" the colonel asked bluntly.

"Revenge," Cole answered. "You destroyed my dreams of being somebody when you gave the job to Clint. And on top of that, this little missy here gave him her heart. Ain't no amount of gold or money going to fix that. Blood is the only fix there is for that," Cole growled.

As Cole was talking, Amber Lynn had managed to grab a
small knife from the counter. She spun to her left and plunged
it into Cole's shoulder as hard as she could.

"Ahhh!" Cole screamed in pain. He shoved her backwards
into the stove, and at the same time he fired his gun at the
colonel, striking him dead center in his chest. The colonel fell
with a thud on the kitchen floor. Grease from the frying pan
splashed onto Amber Lynn's dress, and it burst into flames.
Cole spun around, dropped his gun, grabbed the table cloth
and tried to extinguish the flames, but it was no use. The
flames were now swirling around her head and had engulfed
her entire body. She broke away from him and stumbled
about the room. In a panic, he rushed outside. He could hear
Amber Lynn screaming. He looked at the flames through the
window as he stood in front of the house. The screaming had
stopped, but the flames were growing rapidly.

"Cole! Let's go!" a voice yelled from a distance. He had
brought along two accomplices who had been waiting in the
shadows. They rode up with his horse. He hopped on and
they quickly rode away.

"What in the hell happened in there?" one of them asked.
"Where's the gold?"

"Shut the hell up, and let's get out of here!" Cole spat at the
man.

"But you said there would be gold," the man insisted. Cole grabbed for his gun only to realize it wasn't there. Then he remembered he had dropped it in the kitchen. He knew that could be a problem, but it was too late now to retrieve it. As they rode away, the flames continued to grow until they had consumed the entire house, and the smoke from the fire billowed high into the air, blowing off into the horizon.

***

Clint and Dusty had delivered the herd to Fort Lewis, arriving two days early, and had gotten top dollar from the army agent that the colonel and Mr. Pratt had dealt with for years. Overnight, they paid off the men and headed for home. Riding along with them were two men who had volunteered to help guard the gold for extra pay.

Clint had learned that traveling with Dusty was an experience. He wasn't as crazy as he seemed and was, in fact, quite intelligent. The third night out, the four of them were gathered around the campfire, talking.

"So, Dusty, what possessed you to be a cowboy? I mean, to spend your entire life doing this? Haven't you ever wanted to settle down and get married?" Clint inquired.

"Oh, heck no! Who needs a woman when you can look up at the sky and see the untold number of stars. There isn't anything more beautiful than that," Dusty replied.

"The sky?" Clint asked.

"Yeah, the sky has never failed me. Women will. Women change, and it's not always for the better. The sky changes, too, but it never disappoints you. You look up in the sky, and one day there are clouds you can dance on. The next day, it's the prettiest blue. Bluer than any precious stone. Even when it gets black and angry, it has a menacing beauty about it. Then it rains. Rain to wash your sins away, or at least it feels that way. At night, when you lie down to sleep, you look up and realize just how insignificant you are. Yes, sir, Clint, the sky. Who needs a woman when you have the sky? Besides, I learned a long time ago not to mess with fast women or slow horses," Dusty said.

Out in the darkness, there was a loud crack of a twig breaking, and a voice bellowed loudly.

"Don't be foolish. Drop your weapons!" the man in the darkness warned. "If I see either of you move a muscle, both of you will die!" The two men accompanying him pulled their guns and pointed them at Clint and Dusty.

"Well, ain't this some shit!" Dusty said. "You two no account sons of bitches are in on this?"
The man with the gravelly voice walked in from the darkness. He was a big man, gruff and mean looking, with a scar running up his left jawline. He was pointing a rifle at Clint.

"You're one of the men who rode with us. You helped us bring the herd in," Clint said to the man.

"So I did. What of it?" the man growled.

"What do you want?" Clint asked.

"I'm going to make this simple. You give me the gold, and I don't kill you. That simple enough?"

Clint and Dusty looked at each other. The man with the gravelly voice motioned with his rifle and spoke again, talking to one of his accomplices. "Go look in the saddlebags," he instructed the man. The man went over to Clint's horse, opened the saddlebag and stuck his hand inside. You could hear the gold coins jingling around inside the bag.

"There's lots of gold in here," the man said, looking in the bag.

"See, that wasn't hard now, was it? Take their guns," the man with the rifle told the other man, who quickly grabbed the two six shooters off the ground. He then stepped over and picked up Clint's holster. He pulled the second six shooter out of it and tossed all three guns into the darkness.

"How about you, fat man? You got a second gun hidden in that blubber somewhere?" the rifle man asked Dusty.

"Go to hell," Dusty replied.

"Oh, I'm sure I will, but not today. Search him," the big man told the other man.

As the accomplice began to search him, Dusty pulled a knife out of his shirt sleeve.

"No!" Clint yelled, but it was too late. The man with the gravelly voice fired his rifle, and Dusty stumbled backwards against the chuck wagon, falling to the ground, dead.

"You didn't have to kill him, you son of a bitch!" Clint shouted.

The man with the rifle swung towards Clint and snarled, "You got anything else to say? Don't get any bright ideas, or I'll shoot you, too!" he barked. Clint said nothing as the man approached him. "I didn't think so," he commented, then quickly swung the rifle butt around, striking Clint in the head with it.

Down he went, unconscious.

CHAPTER THIRTEEN

Clint awoke, lying on the ground with the sun on his face. His
head was bloodied, and it hurt even more as he rose to his
feet. Before him was the lifeless body of Dusty. He staggered
over to it, fell to his knees, and began to cry. He found a
shovel on the chuck wagon and started to dig. His tears mixed
with his sweat. The ground was hard, but he refused to leave
his friend's body for the scavengers. His sorrow soon turned
to anger. He could see the men's faces, forever etched in his
memory. Clint would find these men. He was not going to
turn his cheek to this. When the hole was deep enough, he
gathered a blanket, wrapped Dusty up in it as best he could,
and tied both ends with rope. It looked like a shroud but
would suffice as a coffin. He placed Dusty in the hole and
then covered him.

Clint crossed his arms and tried to think of the proper words.
He had read numerous books at the colonel's house, yet he
couldn't think of any that would honor Dusty enough. Then it
came to him. An old Irish blessing he had learned from his
pappy. He repeated it now over Dusty's grave:

> May the road rise up to meet you
> May the wind be always at your back
> May the sunshine be warm upon your face
> And the rains fall soft upon your fields
> Until we meet again

May God hold you in the palm of His hand

With Dusty tended to, Clint went in search of the guns the man had tossed into the darkness the night before. He found them after a few minutes of searching, cleaned them off, and made sure they were loaded.

Clint tied the horses to the chuck wagon and rode towards home. He had lost the gold. Dusty was dead. He had failed drastically. His life was surely over. It took him weeks but he finally reached the ranch. He rode up, staring in disbelief. His mind could not comprehend what his eyes saw. The charred remains of the house was more than he could bear. He stepped off the chuck wagon and ran through the grounds like a madman. The stables, his cabin, the bunk house, all empty.

"Colonel! Amber Lynn!" he kept calling, over and over. The place was abandoned. There was no one to tell him what had happened, no one to tell him where the colonel and Amber Lynn were.

He rode into town, looking for answers. His first stop was the sheriff's office. If anyone knew where they were, it would be Sheriff Franklin. He entered the office, and the sheriff stood up. Clint wasted no time.

"Where are the colonel and Amber Lynn, Sheriff Franklin?" Sheriff Franklin had a narrow face, with deep set eyes and a mean look, even when he smiled. Today, he wasn't smiling at all.

"I'm sorry to have to tell you this, Clint, but they didn't make it out of the fire," he said. Clint's heart sank. His knees became weak so he sat down in a chair. Tears began to blur his vision.

"I don't know what to say," the sheriff stated, for lack of any comforting words.

"You can start by telling me how it happened," Clint coughed out between stifled sobs.

"No one knows. It was late in the evening. One of the townfolk saw the glow. We figured it was coming from the colonel's place, considering the direction and all. By the time we got out there, it was totally on fire. There was nothing we could do but watch it burn. At first, we didn't know if anyone was in the house. It wasn't until afterwards that we, well, found them. We buried their remains in the cemetery. We couldn't tell who was who." The sheriff shared the gruesome details as best he could. Clint's hands were trembling, and the tears flowed like rain down his cheeks.

"There's something else you need to know," the sheriff said. Clint looked up, shaking, his eyes asking the question, "What?"

"The ranch... it now belongs to someone else," the sheriff stated. The news hit Clint like lightning strike and thunderclap combined.

"What? How did that happen?" Clint looked at the sheriff in utter disbelief.

"I don't know the details. You should ask the bank that question," the sheriff suggested. Clint stood, wiped his face, and without looking at the sheriff, walked out the door.

"Clint, I am truly sorry. They were very close friends of mine as you know," he said to Clint's back as he left.

During the walk to the bank, Clint's sorrow mixed with anger. When he entered the bank, Mr. Gleeson, the bank president, looked up as if he was expecting him. The entire staff watched Clint in silence as he walked across the floor to the president's office, walked in, and slammed the door behind him.

"Clint, I'm so sorry for your loss. I—"

Clint cut off the conversation before it even got started.

"I didn't come here for condolences," he said angrily. "Tell me, and tell me right now, how someone else has gained possession of the colonel's ranch!"

Mr. Gleeson, a thin beady-eyed man, sat behind his desk, wringing his hands. He looked at Clint, then the floor, and back at Clint, before he started talking.

"I'm not supposed to talk with you about bank business or the colonel's business, you not being an heir of his or a direct family member," he started to explain, "but since I know the special relationship you had with him and his niece, well, I figure it's the least I can do, in light of the tragedy that has befallen you and the colonel's extended family."

"Get on with it," Clint snarled.

"Um… yes… ahh… The colonel took out a loan on the ranch," Mr. Gleeson said finally.

"A loan? A loan for what?" Clint challenged him.

"To buy more land. He used his ranch as collateral. Said something about the land being a gift. He was going to pay off the loan with the proceeds from the cattle sale in Colorado," Mr. Gleeson shared.

"Why didn't you just take the land he bought with the loan?" Clint asked.

"It's a bit more complicated than that. He made some legal entanglements that forced us to take it all."

"How did the ranch end up in someone else's hands? And whose hands are they?" Clint demanded.

"A Mr. Elks owns it now. With the colonel and his niece gone, the loan went into default. Mr. Elks paid it off. It's just business, and it was all legal, Clint, I assure you," Mr. Gleeson stated confidently.

"Mr. Gleeson, may I ask you a question?" Clint quietly inquired.

"Of course."

"Who owns the biggest share of this bank?"

Why, Mr. Elks does," Mr. Gleeson answered sheepishly.

"That's what I figured. Yeah, just business and all legal. Still doesn't make it right," Clint said as he stormed out of the bank.

Clint next went to the cemetery. He wept bitter tears as he knelt by their graves. How and why were just two of the thoughts racing through his head as he grieved for his friend and his fiancée. His loss was profound. The wife he would never have. The child he would never see. The years they would never have together. The father figure he had lost. When he had no more tears to shed, he bid farewell. "Until we see each other again," he said. As he walked away and mounted his horse, he kept repeating the phrase 'until we see each other again,' over and over, again and again.

Clint returned to the ranch. He sat there on a charred stump, staring at the remains of the home. They're dead. All dead. The colonel, Amber Lynn, the baby he would never know, and Dusty. How could it be? The home where he had learned, laughed, and loved was gone. Why? How? His heart was filled with overwhelming grief. He stood up and walked through the rubble, looking for any remnants of the life he had known, looking for anything that might tell him why his life had vanished. He kicked through the ashes. Then he saw it. The skeleton of a hand gun. He picked it up and wiped off the black soot. There it was, a name engraved on the side of the barrel. Cole.

The fire that consumed the house ran up his arm, into his body, and into his heart. Everything that had been lost had instantly been replaced with something ugly. A desire to spill the blood of another. He felt a monster growing out of his soul. Like a weed pushing up through hard clay, it had to be fed. Clint was going to kill Cole, just as sure as the angels in heaven serve God.

Clint stormed through the door of the sheriff's office, tossing the remnants of the gun on the sheriff's desk.

"What's this?" Sheriff Franklin asked.

"It's what's left of a gun that belonged to a man by the name of Cole, Thomas Cole. He used to work for the colonel. I found it in the ruins of the house. He has to know what happened. He was there during the fire. I know it. His name is engraved on the barrel, for God's sake," Clint said, gritting his teeth.

"Whoa, Clint. You're drawing a lot of conclusions without a lot of proof. How do you know he didn't just leave it there by chance one day?"

"What man leaves his gun behind? Besides, he was forbidden to go on the ranch. He was there, Sheriff, I know it. He probably started the fire!"

"Clint, I know you're upset, but I can't just go and arrest a man for a burned up gun. I would need more proof."

"More proof? Well, I don't need more proof!" Clint snarled and turned and headed out the door.

"Now, Clint, don't go taking the law into your own hands now, you hear?" the sheriff called after him.

Clint asked about town, and found out that Cole had gone to work for Mr. Elks, the man who now owned the colonel's ranch. He quickly rode towards the Elks ranch.

Mr. Elks was a land hungry German immigrant who had come to this country to seek his fortune and was doing it through intimidation and legal wrangling. When Clint reached the outskirts of the Elks ranch, he was stopped by two men who claimed to work there. They were sitting on a wagon in the middle of the road, blocking the way. One of them spat tobacco as Clint rode up. He was cradling a rifle in his lap. The other one was a rough-looking man wearing a single black-handled six shooter and holding the reins in his hands.

"What's your business here?" he asked Clint.

"I'm looking for a man who works here. His name is Cole, Thomas Cole," Clint practically spat out his name.

"I've heard the name. He hired on several months ago. I don't know him personally. What do you want with him?" the man asked.

"That's between him and me," Clint replied curtly.

"Well, mister, we don't just let anyone come riding onto the ranch for no good reason, so I suggest you just mosey on along."

"Look, I'm going on this ranch to find Cole if I have to go around you or through you. Either way, I'm going, and you're not going to like what happens if you try to stop me," Clint said as he touched his pistols.

The men saw the anger and determination in Clint 's eyes and knew that he was serious. Whatever this man wanted with Cole could not be good, but it wasn't worth dying for.

"Well, now, if it's that important, we'll take you," the driver suggested.

The two men in the wagon escorted Clint up to the ranch house where Mr. Elks was seated on the front porch, reading some papers. On each side of him was an armed guard.

"Who is this? And what does he want?" Mr. Elks asked.

Clint wasn't about to put up with this tomfoolery and interjected, "I'm Clint Cain, and I'm looking for Thomas Cole," he said curtly. Mr. Elks looked at Clint with contempt. He said nothing for a moment, then he spoke.

"You must be the Clint Cain I've heard about," he commented, his words thick with a German accent. "Why are you looking for this Cole, may I ask?" It was more of a demand than a request.

"Because I'm going to kill him and anyone who stands in my way." Clint didn't mince his words. Mr. Elks smirked at Clint for a moment, then stopped and got deadly serious.

"You have a lot of nerve, Mr. Cain, coming here like this. Yes, you must have, how you say in America, big balls." Mr. Elks chuckled this time for a moment, then got serious once more.

"I can use a man like you, with big balls." He chuckled again, and Clint interrupted him.

"Is he here?" Clint asked, undeterred. Mr. Elks now looked angry. He obviously wasn't used to being interrupted.

"Cole is not here. He left a couple of weeks ago. Now get off my land before I have you buried in it. Do not darken my door again."

"Did he say where he was going?" Clint asked, not finished with his business.

"Are you deaf, Mr. Cain? I am done with you. Now leave," Mr. Elks snapped.

"I'll leave when my questions are answered, and not before," Clint snapped back. The two bodyguards took a step forward. Fast as lightning, Clint drew his gun and pointed it directly at Mr. Elks. "Go ahead, make a move. The first person I shoot is Mr. Elks here, and then you two. I may be killed by one of these other varmints," Clint said, referring to the two men who had escorted him, "but you'll be dead long before I will." He stared at Mr. Elks, now looking alarmed by the turn of events.

"Let's not be too hasty, Mr. Cain," Mr. Elks remarked as he shifted nervously in his chair.

"Where did Cole go?" Clint asked curtly.

"He said he was going to go to Colorado," Mr. Elks offered.

"Did he say where in Colorado?" Clint pressed.

"He said he had a friend near Fort Lewis he had to pay a visit to—an old friend," Mr. Elks informed Clint.

"A couple of weeks ago?"

"About the time of the fire at the Billups ranch," Mr. Elks shared.

"Speaking of the Billups ranch—" Clint started, but Mr. Elks cut him off.

"First and foremost, young man, I had nothing to do with the demise of the colonel and his niece. He was a good man, an honest man. Sure, I wanted his land and the land he outbid me for, but I would never resort to killing a man for his land. And especially not a young woman who had nothing to do with our rivalry. There are so many other things I could have done, financially, to force his hand. You have my sympathy, and my condolences." Mr. Elks sounded sincere enough. "Secondly, I do not appreciate you coming here like this, making threats. I'll have to speak to the sheriff about this." Mr. Elks was still so self-centered and so full of self-importance that he thought he was in charge.

Clint gave him a cold-blooded stare, and Mr. Elks knew Clint wasn't amused by his admonishment. He once more shifted nervously in his chair, breaking off eye contact. After a moment, Clint turned his horse northwest towards Colorado and rode away.

CHAPTER FOURTEEN

Clint owed Cole a debt of revenge, and he was going to pay that debt. He was going to deliver his own kind of justice and make it stick. It made sense that Cole would leave the Elks ranch, knowing that Clint would be returning soon, but as he rode, something about the timeline stuck in his mind. A couple of weeks ago, or could it have been few weeks ago? Clint knew the fire happened just about a week before they had reached Fort Lewis with the cattle. A man with a fast horse or two horses could ride all out and reach Fort Lewis in about a week, maybe a little less. He knew that Cole was running like a rabbit being chased by a dog, and he was going to find him even if he had to follow him into hell.

When he arrived in Fort Lewis, he learned that yes, Cole had been there, but he and three other men had moved on the day before Clint had arrived. It seems they had plenty of money and had been living high on the hog while they were there. With a little effort, Clint found out Cole and his buddies had headed for Dodge City, Kansas, a week's ride from Fort Lewis.

Clint took the high ground, riding at night looking for campfires, and sleeping for short periods of time during the day. After four days on their trail, Clint spotted a campfire next to the Arkansas River, a day's ride from Dodge City. He had no way of knowing if it was Cole, but something in his gut told him it was, so he rode towards it.

He left his horse a hundred yards out and snuck up to the campsite. He could see three men in the firelight but couldn't make out their faces. As he got closer, he heard Cole's voice as he walked in from the darkness on the opposite side of the campfire. He was tucking in his shirt, apparently just having relieved himself. Clint waited until Cole was sitting down again and then stood up and walked into the camp, both guns in his hands.

"The first man to make a false move will be the first man to die," Clint said from the darkness.
After a moment, when nobody moved, Clint issued his next order. "Now, carefully and slowly remove your gun belts. Don't get up. Take them off right where you're at."

"But I'm sitting on mine," one of the men said.

"You'll just have wiggle around a bit to get it off then, won't you? Of course, you stand up and I could shoot you. Yeah, that sounds good. Problem solved," Clint said with just a hint of sarcasm.

As they dropped their belts, Clint came out of the shadows and stood off to the side of the campfire where he had them in direct line of sight. Cole looked at Clint as if he were looking at a ghost.

"Clint, what brings you all the way out here in the middle of the night to the middle of Kansas?" he asked nervously as if he didn't know.

"I just went out for some fresh air and found my way here. Imagine that," Clint replied sarcastically. "Say, don't I know you three?" Clint stated, his eyes locked on the others.

"Hell if I know. We get around a lot," said a big man with a scar running down his left jawline. Clint looked closely at the other two and recognized them also. They were the cowpokes who had volunteered to ride back to Texas with Dusty and him. He knew, right then, they were in this deep, right up to their eyebrows as Cole's partners.

"Clint, what's this all about, anyway? We weren't bothering anyone." Cole did a poor job deterring the wrath about to be unleashed against him.

"If you need a few dollars, we can help you out," one of the other men said, and Clint snapped at him immediately.

"You think this is about money? You think you can buy me off by giving me a little of my own money back?" Clint was becoming enraged by these thieves and murderers. "You had no trouble shooting down my friend and stealing the gold I was charged with safekeeping. But now that the shoe is on the other foot, you haven't even the courage to stand there and keep your mouth shut. I have half a mind to shoot where you stand," Clint snarled and glared at the man. In the corner of his eye, he saw the big man move. He was reaching for his rifle, and Clint couldn't have that.

Clint spun quickly to his left and fired one shot, striking the big man in the neck. The man hollered in pain, grabbing at his neck as he fell to his knees. The other man who had been hired to ride with Clint and Dusty back to the ranch dove for his gun. He actually managed to reach it and roll over to where he could fire, but Clint was well ahead of him and shot him dead. The man did manage to fire off his gun, but he missed Clint by a good yard and instead shot his friend, who was standing next to him.

Clint spun back to face Cole who had started to lean over, but stopped when he realized Clint had spun back to face him.

"I don't think so, Cole," Clint growled, and Cole quickly raised his hands again.

"You got this all wrong, old friend. I don't even know these guys. We just met the other day on the trail," Cole said, grasping at straws.

"Really. Then the men in Fort Lewis were lying when they said you and these cow turds were living it up in the saloon," Clint replied as he stared hard at Cole, who was fidgeting under his glare.

"They must have me confused with some other cowboy," Cole suggested as he looked around for something, anything, he could use to defend himself.

"They knew you by name, Cole. They knew you by name," Clint informed him.

"No, I tell you, it wasn't me," Cole insisted.

"And those cow turds planned on robbing Dusty and me, with some inside information provided by you."

"No, I didn't have anything to do with that. You've got to believe me, Clint. I wouldn't do that to you," Cole whined loudly.

"Weren't you the one who stood there at the colonel's and vowed to make us pay for you not getting the foreman's job, saying how I stole your woman, and that you'd make us sorry we treated you that way?" Clint said.

"I was drunk, and I was angry. I didn't know what I was saying!"

"Then you weren't there when the ranch burned?" Clint asked.

"What? The ranch burned? When did that happen? Is everyone okay?"

"So, you had nothing to do with the fire then?" Clint asked him, and again, Cole lied to try and save his ass.

"No! I didn't even know anything about it until you just told me. It must be bad, otherwise why would you be here? But I didn't do it. I'll tell you what, though, I'll help you find the men who did," Cole offered. Then he added, "The gold those men stole from you, at least what's left of it, is in their saddle bags."

Clint placed his right gun back in its holster, reached into his pocket, pulled something out, and tossed it at Cole's feet. Cole stood there, looking back and forth between Clint and the item wrapped in a rag at his feet.

"Pick it up," Clint demanded.

Slowly, Cole bent over, picked it up, and unwrapped it. He looked at it, shaking. It was the remnants of his gun. The one he had dropped at the Billups ranch. He looked up at Clint, almost knowing that he was going to die. But he said nothing.

"Explain that," Clint demanded. Cole shifted on his wobbly legs and started to say something, but stopped.

"You can't, can you? You killed the colonel, Amber Lynn, and my unborn child. Were you drunk then, too? Are you drunk now?" Clint barked at Cole, who had the look of caged rabbit.

"Put on your gun," Clint ordered. "I'm giving you a chance. More of a chance than you gave the colonel and Amber, I'll bet," he snarled as he set his other gun back in its holster.

Cole dropped the remnants of his old gun on the ground. He then took a step to his right and reached down for his gun belt. As he grabbed it, he seized it by the gun's butt, slipped his finger through the trigger guard, and fired at Clint as he swung the gun up in his direction.

Clint immediately fired off a round, striking Cole in the upper chest. But Cole had hit Clint in the upper left shoulder. Clint staggered back a few steps and fired again, hitting Cole a second time, this time in the gut. He stood there watching Cole, who was now on his knees, clutching at his chest and gut with both hands. Clint slowly walked towards him, stopping a foot in front of him, oblivious to his own pain.

"You done killed me, Clint!" Cole said, gurgling blood and looking up. "For God's sake, help me," he moaned.

"God's not here. I feel no charity towards you. I'll leave you to the buzzards. You don't deserve a Christian burial. May God show you no mercy and send you to hell for eternity," Clint told him.

Clint raised his foot and kicked Cole squarely in the face, sending him flat on his back. He then raised his weapon and fired it, striking Cole between the eyes. Cole's body jerked then became perfectly still, with his lifeless eyes wide open, staring at the night sky.

Clint went to the dead men's horses, collected the saddlebags with the colonel's gold in them, and put them all on one horse.

He then gathered all the guns and gun belts, placing them on another horse. Then he tied the horses together in a string, mounted the lead one, and rode off towards an uncertain future. All he knew was that he was done being a cowboy and was ready for whatever the future sent his way.

R

Made in the USA
Middletown, DE
20 October 2017